DON QUIXOTE

DON QUIXOTE

Miguel de Cervantes

Bloomsbury Books
London

This edition published 1993 by Bloomsbury Books, an imprint
of The Godfrey Cave Group, 42 Bloomsbury Street, London,
WC1B 3QJ.

ISBN 1 85471 255 1

Printed and bound by Imprimerie Hérissey, France.
N° d'impression : 24967

CONTENTS

PART 1

PART 2

PART 1

1

How Don Quixote rode out

In one of the villages of La Mancha, in the country of Spain, there dwelt many years ago a gentleman named Quixada. He was nearer fifty than forty years of age, tall and strong, with a long, lanky body, and a lantern-jawed face, as his name implied. Like many another gentleman of his class he kept a horse and a hound, a lance on a rack and a target on the wall, wore velvet on Sundays and homespun on weekdays, lived frugally, was an early riser and an enthusiastic sportsman. His family consisted of a middle-aged housekeeper and his own niece, who was not quite twenty.

He had a passion for reading, and for reading of a particular kind. He knew no greater delight than to sit conning books of romance and chivalry, tales of high adventure and gallant deeds of knight-errantry, encounters of heroes and giants, and all the marvellous actions of the legendary warriors of old. The more he read, the more he longed to read; he was, as it were, steeped in books of chivalry; yet he gave ever more and more time to this, his best-loved pursuit. He even gave up coursing and hunting, and sold many good acres of his land in order to buy for himself more volumes of romance, in which for days together he would bury himself, blind and deaf to all around him.

The good priest of his parish was a great friend of
Señor Quixada's, and the two would have many a long
talk about the knights of old-time legends and their
adventures, and many a warm dispute about the re-
spective merits of the gallant Palmerin of England and
the notable Amadis de Gaul. As time went on, Señor
Quixada's head became more and more full of tales of
chivalry, which he read literally from sunrise to sunset, and from sunset to sunrise again; until, what with
far too little sleep and far too much reading, his mind
became quite crazed upon this subject, though upon
other matters he was as sane as his neighbours and a
good deal wiser than some of them.

His brain was so filled with high notions of chivalry
and romance that very soon he became possessed with
one of the oddest ideas that a freakish wit ever devised. He decided that he would take horse and lance,
armour and target, and, thus equipped after the fashion
of the knights of old, go forth, like them, to wander
over the world, to right all wrongs, to relieve the distressed, to uphold the weak, to put down abuses, and
generally to seek heroic adventures such as those nar-
rated in his books of romance.

The first thing he did was to bring out a suit of
mouldy, rusty armour that had belonged to his great-
great-grandfather. This he scoured and freshened as
well as he could, and then, finding that there was no
helmet, but a simple steel cap, he set to work to make
a visor out of pasteboard. The visor made the cap into
a most presentable looking helmet; but it was not so

strong as it appeared to be, as he very soon found, when, drawing his sword to test its powers of resistance, he broke it with two strokes, thereby undoing a week's work in a second's time. However, he mended it to his satisfaction, though he did not care to test it again; and he thought it would now serve its purpose excellently.

Next he thought of his horse, a good, hard working beast, as gaunt and lanky and bony as its master. But Quixada was of the opinion that no beast in all the records of history or romance, no, not Alexander's famed Bucephalus himself, was the equal of this steed of his. Seeing that he himself was to become a knight-errant, he wished to give his horse a name that might fit its master's high condition—a name that would sound well, yet at the same time express what the animal had been before it became the charger of a gallant knight. Four days did Señor Quixada rack his brain for a suitable title, and at last he fixed upon the name of Rosinante (*rocin* meaning a drudge horse, and *ante* signifying before), and this he considered very satisfactory indeed.

He took eight more days to ponder over a name for himself, and at length decided that he would henceforth be known by the title of Don Quixote. Then he remembered the famed Amadis de Gaul and other knights of old who had added their country's name to their own and glorified it thereby; he made up his mind to do the same, calling himself from that time *Don Quixote de la Mancha*.

Having now provided himself with armour, a horse, and a new name, he cast about in his mind for some suitable lady who was to be the lovely object of his adoration and his vows. For he knew very well that all the famous knights he had read of had ever been devoted to some particular lady—indeed, a knight-errant without one was no better than a tree without leaves, or a body without a soul. So our good and gallant Don Quixote bethought himself of a simple country lass who lived not far from his village. He had once been in love with her, though the damsel knew nothing at all of the matter, and, even if she knew him, had never given a second's thought to him or his concerns. Her name was Aldonza Lorenzo, but this name was not sufficiently high-sounding or romantic for her adoring knight. He gave her the name of Dulcinea, after a charming shepherdess in one of his books of romance; and as she was born, and lived, in Toboso, from that very hour she became, in the thoughts of Don Quixote, the beauteous, pitiless, and high-born Lady Dulcinea del Toboso.

Behold, then, one glorious hot July morning, Don Quixote sallying forth in quest of adventures, lance in hand, target on arm, arrayed in his helmet and armour, and mounted upon Rosinante. But he had hardly got out upon the open plain (by way of a back door in his garden wall) when a most disturbing thought came suddenly into his mind. He had not yet been dubbed a knight, according to the laws of chivalry! If he had not received the honour of knighthood, how could he per-

form the worthy deeds of that order? Then, again, sup-
posing he were knighted, he knew that a new knight
must wear white armour, with no device upon his arms
until he had earned one by his prowess. But he presently comforted himself by deciding that he would beg
for knighthood at the hands of the first person whom
he should meet; and as for his armour, he meant to
scour that until it should appear whiter than ermine.

So he rode along, almost bursting with pleasure and
pride at the thought of his valiant deeds that were yet
to come, and the name which he should thereby make
for himself in the records of chivalry. And then he
called aloud upon his absent lady Dulcinea, beseeching her not to be so cruel as to withhold her favour
from him who was so enslaved by her loveliness, and
who endured so many afflictions for her sake. For in
this manner, he knew right well, every knight of old
had addressed the lady of his heart.

All that day he rode without meeting with any adventure, and at nightfall, weary and hungry, he came
to a roadside inn. Two country lasses lolled at the inn-
door, and Don Quixote, who coloured all that he saw,
or thought, or experienced, with the extravagant romance out of his books, immediately decided that the
frowzy inn was a magnificent embattled castle, and
that the girls were two noble ladies who were taking
the evening air at the castle gates.

He drew rein before them, therefore; but the damsels, scared at the sight of the tall, thin, weird figure,
with its lance and buckler, began to draw back hastily

into the house. Whereupon Don Quixote lifted up his visor of pasteboard, and said with great gravity and courtesy:

"Fly not from me, I beseech you, gentle ladies: you may fear no incivility whatever from me. For I profess the noble order of knighthood, which permits me to harm nothing that is harmless, much less such noble and beauteous damsels as you most certainly are."

The two girls stared until their eyes almost fell out, so odd was the stranger's appearance, and so unusual his speech. At length they both burst out laughing loudly—a breach of good behaviour which irritated Don Quixote, and caused him to rebuke them gravely.

"Let me tell you, ladies," he said with some severity, "that modesty and civility become all, but more especially maidens such as yourselves; and to laugh immoderately at that which is no subject for mirth ever displays a foolishness and shallowness of mind. However, I do not wish you to take my words amiss, for I only desire to honour and serve you in all things."

But the damsels only giggled the more at his stately words, and Don Quixote's wrath was rapidly rising when the innkeeper appeared. He was too portly and lazy a fellow to be anything but peaceable, and, though amazed and inwardly much entertained at his new guest's appearance and speech (for the Don, taking him to be no other than the worthy governor of the supposed castle, addressed him as such), he invited him into the inn, and helped him down from his horse.

"I pray you, Señor Castellano," said Don Quixote,

as he alighted stiffly, "to have especial care taken of my gallant Rosinante, for he is one of the finest chargers that ever ate corn."

The innkeeper, looking over poor Rosinante's bony carcass, had his own opinion about that; but he led the horse away to the stable, and, when he returned to the inn-kitchen, found the two lasses—who had recovered from their fit of shyness and giggling—charming the guest. His steel back- and breast-pieces were already laid aside, but the girls could not unfasten his gorget, nor were they able to free him from his make-shift visor, which he had secured very tightly and securely with green ribbons. Nothing would persuade him to have the ribbons cut, so that he was obliged to keep his helmet on.

They brought him food by and by—coarse black bread and some little dried fishes, but he was quite unable to feed himself because of his cumbersome helmet and beaver. So the damsels, like birds feeding their young, put every morsel of food into his mouth. Then the innkeeper placed one end of a hollow reed between the Don's lips, and through the other end he gently poured as much wine as his guest was able to drink. The figure that Don Quixote cut in this situation was absurd enough to make the gravest laugh, but he bore the operation without a smile or a complaint, so determined was he not to part from his beloved visor.

He had already told the girls and the innkeeper his name and quality; and when, soon after, he heard a swineherd sounding his pipe of reeds outside, he was more certain than ever that he was in some stately castle, that the swineherd's pipe was a herald's summons, that the damsels were noble ladies, and the innkeeper the governor of the fortress. The food he ate was, to his romantic mind, no less than dainty white bread and delicate trout; and, considering all these things, he was perfectly satisfied that his adventure had begun very well indeed. But there was still one matter which troubled him, and this was, that he had not yet been dubbed a knight.

2

How Don Quixote was made a Knight

When Don Quixote had ended his supper, he bade the host follow him to the stable, and there, shutting the door, he fell on his knees before him.

"I will never rise from this place, valiant knight," cried he, "if you will not at once consent to grant me a boon which, in the granting, will honour you and benefit all the human race besides."

The innkeeper stared, and, not knowing what else to do, would have helped the other to his feet, but this the Don would by no means permit until his host had promised him what he asked. The promise being given, Don Quixote stood up and said:

"I expected as much, sir, from your honourable and courteous behaviour. And now, the boon which I desire, and which you have this moment granted, is nothing less than that you shall tomorrow bestow the glorious order of knighthood upon me. This night I will faithfully watch my armour in the chapel of your castle here, and tomorrow, of your grace and courtesy, I beg that you will dub me true knight, that I may properly set forth, after the fashion of all knights, upon my heroic quest, to ease the distressed and wander the world over in search of high adventures which will glorify my name in future ages."

The host had already had his suspicions of the Don's soundness of mind, but now, being quite convinced that he was crazy, he determined to indulge his whim and make some mirth at his expense. He therefore told him that he approved of his resolve, and that next morning the ceremony of knighting should take place with all due observances. But he added, that as the chapel of his castle had been pulled down, his honourable guest might very fittingly watch his arms in the court of his castle (meaning the inn-yard).

He then asked Don Quixote whether he carried any money with him.

"Not a maravedi," replied the would-be knight, "and, indeed, I never heard, or read, that any other knights-errant ever had any either."

"Oh, I assure you that you are mistaken, worthy sir," answered the other; "perhaps you have not heard or read of such things, because they have ever been taken as a matter of course and so not mentioned; but a supply of money and of clean shirts is, I know right well, the regular outfit of a knight-errant. And these form part of the baggage which should properly be carried by his squire."

Don Quixote promised to observe all this; and very soon after, began to keep the vigil beside his arms in the inn-yard. He had laid his armour upon a horse-trough there, and now, with his buckler upon his arm and his lance in his hand, he began to pace gravely to and fro before it with much deliberation.

All the folk of the inn came out by and by, and stood

at a distance to watch the gaunt figure in the moon-light, now moving with slow and stately steps, now pausing, apparently lost in thought, before the pile of armour, gazing upon it earnestly.

An hour or two went by, whilst the inn-folk watched and whispered and the Don guarded his armour, seem-ingly unaware of anything else in the world. At last, a carrier came into the yard to water his mules. In order to do this he had of course to lift the arms from the trough, and he was just about to do so when Don Quixote awoke from his long reverie and saw him.

"Hold, rash knight, whoever thou art!" he cried. "For know that no man, save on pain of death, shall lay so much as a finger on the arms of the worthiest and bravest adventurer who ever girded sword on thigh!"

The carrier, however, took not the slightest notice of this threat; instead, he gathered up the armour from the trough and pitched it noisily into the middle of the yard. Whereupon Don Quixote slipped off his buckler, took his lance in both hands, and brought it down with terrific force upon the intruder's head. He fell like a log, nor was there need of a second blow to quieten him, which was, perhaps, as well, for another such stroke had put him beyond the aid of any surgeon.

Don Quixote gave no further heed to him, but calmly picked up his arms, arranged them again upon the horse-trough, and resumed his slow and solemn march to and fro.

Presently a second carrier arrived, and, needing wa-ter for his beasts, would have dealt with the armour as the first man had done. But this time the Don, without speaking a word, once more lifted his lance and gave the meddler such a blow that he likewise fell down stunned, with a sorely cracked crown.

But at this second deed of valour, a great hubbub arose among the carrier's comrades and the folk of the inn. They poured into the yard, shouting threats and abuses; and Don Quixote, seeing them, drew his sword and loudly challenged them to do their worst. A volley of stones answered him, but he gallantly stood his ground beside his armour, defending himself with his buckler. The host bawled to the assailants to forbear; and the Don faced them so undauntedly, and presented so dreadful and fantastic an appearance as he stood there, that by and by they quailed before him and at last slunk away. Then, as if nothing had happened, the future knight quietly returned to his vigil.

The innkeeper, by no means relishing this disturbance at his house, resolved to get rid of the cause of it as soon as he decently could. He therefore went up to the Don, and humbly begged his pardon for the rough and uncivil treatment he had received. He then went on to say that, as he had told the Don before, there was no chapel in his castle where arms might be watched, but that his worship had already performed that duty for a sufficient length of time: he had been at it above four hours, and such a vigil really required only two. Then he said that the most important part of the ceremony of knighting was without doubt the blows upon the neck and shoulders, and this he had learned might be performed anywhere, even in the open air. So that, if his noble guest pleased, he would knight him there and then without any further delay.

Don Quixote consented, and the host went to fetch a greasy account book in which the scores of the inn were entered and reckoned up. When he returned he had the two lasses with him, as well as a little scrub of a boy carrying a candle end to give light to the ceremony.

The innkeeper ordered Don Quixote to kneel down, and then began to mumble a mock ritual from his book. Presently he struck him smartly upon the nape of the neck with his hand, and afterwards upon the shoulder with the Don's own sword, muttering all the time from the book he held.

Then he told one of the damsels to gird on the knight's sword, which she did with many a stifled chuckle, and several winks and nods to her companion. But none dared let their mirth be seen, or raise any objections to the Don's whimsies, for no one cared to make another trial of his prowess.

The other damsel fastened on the knight's spurs, and thus the ceremony ended. Don Quixote made many elaborate though sincere expressions of thanks and never-ending service to the two ladies. Then he saddled Rosinante, mounted him, bade a most respectful and grateful farewell to his host (who was too thankful to see the last of him to make any charges for food or lodging), and set forth upon his travels again, a full-fledged knight.

He had made up his mind to take the innkeeper's hint, and obtain a supply of money, a change of clothing, and a squire to follow and wait upon him, before he went to seek any further adventures. He therefore turned his horse's head in the direction of his own village; and Rosinante, who knew well enough that he had his face towards his stable, changed his weary amble to what was for him quite a cheerful canter. This pace suited well with his master's mood, for he rode forward rejoicing at every step of his steed, to think that he was actually a knight at last.

After some time, he met a company of riders coming towards him upon the high-road. They proved to be merchants of Toledo who were on the road to Murcia, followed by mounted servants and some muleteers on foot. Don Quixote had no sooner set eyes upon them than he knew what to do—or rather, what would have been the correct proceeding for a former knight of romance—and he acted accordingly.

Taking a firmer hold of his lance and settling himself in his saddle, he held his target before his body, reined Rosinante quite across the highway, and awaited the strangers' coming. Then, when they had drawn nearer to him, he lifted up his voice and called aloud:

"Let the whole world stand, if the whole world will not at once confess that there is not in the whole world a more peerless lady than the lovely empress of La Mancha, Dulcinea del Toboso!"

The merchants stared and gaped at the strange figure and the stranger words, until one waggish gentleman among them spoke for the rest.

"Señor Cavalier," said he courteously, "we have the misfortune not to know the lady whom you name. But if we might see her, we could at once judge of her beauty, and, if she prove as fair as you proclaim her to be, we will confess the truth of that fact, with all our hearts."

"That is not the point," replied the Don hotly. "If you saw her, what merit would there be in confessing what all the world acknowledges? But to believe without seeing—to believe and solemnly swear and maintain—that is the great matter, sir. And if you refuse to do so, I challenge all of you here to combat, either singly or in a body, I care not how, for in a cause as just as this is I defy you one and all!"

"I beseech you, sir," answered the merchant calmly, "not to make us lay a burden upon our consciences by confessing something we know nothing of. But show us a portrait of this lady, if only it be no larger than a barley-corn, and if the face pictured there be all that you say, we are more than willing to acknowledge her peerlessness, guessing at the clue by the thread, as it were. Nay, we are indeed already so far inclined to agree with you, that we will swear she is as fair as you please, even though her portrait show her to be crooked, cross-eyed, or hump-backed."

"Hump-backed!" roared the enraged knight. "Base varlets, my lady is neither hump-backed nor crooked, but as straight and shapely as one of the spindles of Guadarrama! Ah! villains, you shall pay dearly for the blasphemy you have uttered but now!"

And without staying an instant he couched his spear, set spurs to Rosinante, and ran full tilt against the man who had spoken. What the result of such a furious onset would have been we cannot say, had not poor Rosinante unfortunately stumbled and fallen in mid-course, bringing his rider to the earth with a resounding crash. There the unhappy knight lay sprawling, tangled in his stirrups, encumbered by his armour, and quite unable to rise on account of it. But if his limbs were put out of action for the time being, his tongue was not.

"Stay, you scoundrels, stay! Rogues! Slaves!" he bellowed. "Let me once get to my feet, and I will deal with you all! Can ye not see that 'tis through my horse's fault and not through mine that I have been brought to this pass?"

The merchants rode off, laughing; but one of their servants, vexed by the Don's boastful behaviour and determined to repay him for it, came up to him, broke his lance in pieces, and began to belabour him soundly with one of the splinters. His masters called to him to stop, but he gave no heed to them, only laid on with redoubled vigour, pounding the knight almost to a jelly, until he was too exhausted himself to beat his victim any more; and at last he left him.

All this time Don Quixote had never ceased his angry threats and reproaches, in spite of the blows. When he was left alone, he again attempted to rise; but if he found the task hard before, he discovered that it was now an impossible one for him, so bruised and battered was he, and sore and aching in every limb.

He lay for some time in this pitiable plight, until at last a countryman from his own village, leading an ass, passed by the scene of the knight's downfall. He went up to him, and, when he had wiped the dust from his face, knew him at once. He was filled with wonder to find his respectable neighbour in such a condition; but he took off the Don's armour, and helped him upon his ass. Then he collected all our hero's arms, even the splinters of the lance, tied them upon Rosinante, and presently, leading both beasts, set off for home.

He found Don Quixote's house all in an uproar. The priest and the village barber, the knight's two friends, were there; and the Don's niece and his housekeeper were almost beside themselves at the disappearance of the master of the house.

"Alas! alas!" wailed the housekeeper, "neither my master, nor his horse, nor his target, nor his spear, have been seen about the place for the past six days! As sure as I live, 'tis those miserable books of romance which have turned his head, and sent him forth on a gallivant of knight-errantry!"

"It must be so, Master Nicholas," chimed in the niece, addressing the barber, "for my poor uncle was wont to bury himself in those unfortunate books of disadventures from morn to night and from night to morning again, until he would think himself a hero too, and draw his sword, and make passes through the

air, and then say he had slain four giants as tall as
steeples Oh! oh! why did I not tell you and the good
father of all this before? How much trouble it might
have saved! Those wicked books should all be burned!"

"So say I," remarked the priest, "and it is in my
mind to pass judgement upon them all tomorrow, and
condemn them to the flames!"

At this moment the countryman appeared, with the
Don stretched out upon the ass, and then what an outcry there was! All crowded round the knight, his friends
to greet him, his housekeeper and niece to embrace
him in their gladness. They overwhelmed him with
exclamations and eager questions; but he answered
nothing but: "Give me food, and let me get to bed, and
to sleep, for mercy's sake!" Nor would he tell a word
of his adventures until he had had what he required.

3

How the Knight lost his Books and Found a Squire

The priest and the barber questioned the countryman, who told them where and how he had found Don Quixote. And they were more than ever sure that his books of chivalry had turned the knight's head, when the fellow also told them that in spite of his miserable plight the Don had never ceased to recite high-flown passages from romantic stories, both at the time he was found, and all the way home.

Next day, whilst the knight was still a-bed nursing his bruises, the priest asked his niece for the key of his library. She handed it over gladly enough, and then entered the chamber with him, the housekeeper, and the barber. There they found more than a hundred huge volumes, besides a number of smaller ones.

"Hand them to me one by one, Master Nicholas," said the priest, "and I will look over them separately, lest perchance some should be condemned to the flames which do not deserve so hard a fate."

"No, I pray you!" cried the niece eagerly, "do not spare one of them, good father, for they are every one mischief-makers. Throw them all into the yard there, and we will make a bonfire of the lot."

The housekeeper joined her anxious entreaties to

those of the niece; and presently the barber began to hand the books to the priest, who would not, however, have all destroyed without at least scanning the titles.

"What is this?" said his reverence, taking the first one from the barber. *"The History of Amadis de Gaul?* Ah, the first book of chivalry that ever was printed in Spain—the father, as one may say, of all other such books. And therefore, as the leader of so harmful a crew, he should, I think, be sent to the flames without mercy."

"Nay, sir," replied the barber, "but I have heard that it is by far the best of all books of its kind, and thus it ought without doubt to be spared."

"Well, so be it, then," was the priest's answer. "And now, what have we here?"

"The Adventures of Esplandian," said the barber, "who was the son of the renowned Amadis."

"Pah!" replied the priest, "the goodness of the father shall by no means benefit the son. Here, Mistress Housekeeper, take him and throw him out into the yard, as a beginning to the bonfire."

The housekeeper, rejoicing mightily, did as she was bidden, and poor Esplandian was sent flying into the yard, to await his fate.

Thereafter, volume after volume of the knight's cherished collection was handed over to the housekeeper to be burned; and she, to save herself the trouble of going so often to and fro, opened the window and pitched them with a will into the yard beneath.

By and by the priest grew heartily tired of examining every book, and declared that all the rest were worthless, and might be burned along with the others. The housekeeper and the niece made a glorious bonfire that same night, burning all the books that were in both the yard and the house. And some of the volumes that were really worth preserving shared the same fate as the other books, but in the general rout they passed unnoticed, thus proving the truth of the saying that 'the just sometimes suffer for the unjust'.

The priest and the barber decided, that in order to turn Don Quixote's mind from his books of chivalry and his crazy romantic notions, his library should be walled up without delay, so that when he rose from his bed he might not find either books or chamber. For they hoped that when the cause of his wild fancy was gone, the effect would soon go also.

Their orders were carried out; and a few days later Don Quixote got up. Of course, he went at once to find his beloved books. For some time he roamed up and down looking for the chamber which had so mysteriously vanished, and when he came to the place where the door had been, he could do no more than stare and feel about without a word to say. Finally, he asked the housekeeper where his library had gone to. She had her answer ready.

"What library does your worship mean?" said she. "There is neither library nor book in this house now, for the evil one has carried the whole away with him."

"It was not the evil one, either," struck in the niece, "but a dreadful enchanter who came mounted upon a serpent and riding on a cloud, the very day after you went away. He went into your library, and what he did there I cannot say, but when he left, the house was filled with smoke, and when we went to look we could find neither room nor books. And we heard him say, that because of a secret grudge which he bore the owner of it, he had done an act of mischief to this house which should soon be known. And he said, moreover, that his name was Muñaton the Wizard."

"Friston, he meant to say," observed the Don.

"I am sure," said the housekeeper, "I cannot remember whether it was Friston or Friton. I only know that it ended in *ton*."

"Yes, that is so," replied the Don. "He is a powerful enchanter, and one of my worst enemies; for by the aid of his arts he has come to know that one of these days I shall engage in single combat with a favourite knight of his, and that I shall overcome him in spite of all obstacles. And because of this the wizard Friston tries to work me all the ill he can; but every art of his shall avail him nothing: I can outface them all!"

"Who doubts that?" cried the niece. "But oh, dear uncle, why need you thus disturb yourself for nothing? Why cannot you stay at home like a good Christian, and not go wandering up and down the universe seeking for better bread than a wheaten loaf, and, mayhap, like many another body, going out for wool and coming home shorn yourself?"

"Peace, child," replied her uncle, "what do you know of these matters? Let them attempt to shear me—only let them attempt it, I say," he went on in a louder tone of rising anger, "and I vow that I will pluck out all their beards before they shall lay so much as a finger upon one hair of mine!"

For a full fortnight after this conversation Don Quixote stayed quietly at home, without making any effort to indulge in further adventures. But he persuaded a labouring man of his village, a poor, honest, and very simple-minded fellow, to attend him when he should ride forth again, and to serve him as his squire. Sancho Panza, as this man was called, had a wife and family; but the Don talked to him with such pleasing arguments, painted the coming adventures in such glowing colours, and promised him so many great things, that he soon resolved to leave his home and follow him. He was more than ever determined to do this when he heard the knight say that no doubt in a very short time they might have their part in an enterprise wherein an island might be won, and if so, he, Sancho Panza, should most certainly be made the governor of it.

With such-like visions in his mind, Sancho willingly agreed to act as squire to Don Quixote de la Mancha. He promised to be ready upon the appointed day, with all things needful, including a wallet, which Don Quixote charged him by no means to forget, and his own good ass Dapple, upon whose back he intended to follow his master.

Don Quixote was a little disturbed in mind at the mention of the ass: he could not remember ever having read that any gallant knight's squire rode upon an ass before. However, he consoled himself with the resolve that, upon the first opportunity he got, he would unhorse some well-equipped knight upon the road, and so mount his squire upon a better beast.

By means of selling some things and pawning others (and losing more than a little in the business) the Don managed to obtain a sum of money, and such supplies as he required for his second sally into the world beyond his village. He also patched up his helmet once more, and borrowed a buckler from a friend, and, when all things were ready, he rode out of the village unseen one fine night, with Sancho behind him.

The need for secrecy was thought to be great; so that Sancho had taken no farewell of his wife and children, nor had the Don of his friends. They rode with all the speed they could, and by daybreak thought they were safely beyond all pursuit.

Sancho, with his wallet and his leathern wine-bottle, trotted beside his master, his mind full of the island which he believed he was so soon to govern.

"I hope, your worship," he said at last to the knight, "that you have in no way forgot the promise you made to me about that island: I warrant I shall know how to govern it, however large it may be." And he braced his sturdy muscles and swelled his portly body with pride.

"You must know, good friend," replied Don Quixote, "that it was once a well-observed custom for knights to make their squires governors over the islands or kingdoms which they conquered by the force of their arms. But, in their case, this was not until, by time and hardships, the said squires had grown old and worn in their service. Now, I doubt not that I can do better for my squire than that; for it may chance that before six days have gone by I shall conquer a great kingdom that has other kingdoms depending on it. And so, if you live and I live, of one of these kingdoms I promise to make you the king. Nor need you wonder mightily at that, either, for there is no knowing what may happen, and I may easily bestow a good deal more than I promise."

"So, then, if I do indeed come to be a king by one of those strange turns of fortune," said Sancho musingly, "my wife, Teresa Panza, will likewise be a queen, and all my children infantes and infantas?"

"Certainly," answered the knight, "who doubts that?"

"I doubt it," said Sancho, "for I am very sure that if it pleased Heaven to rain down kingdoms upon the earth, not one of them would sit easily upon the head of Teresa Panza, for she is not worth two farthings as a queen. No, no; to be a countess, please your worship, would fit her better, and even with a countessship I doubt her hands would be as full as she could hold."

"Leave all that to Providence, Sancho," replied his master, "for Providence orders all things well for each one of us. Yet you need not content yourself with anything less than a lord-lieutenantship."

"That will be as your honour pleases," answered Sancho dutifully, "for so great a knight as you are, is bound to know best what is the best for me."

4

The Adventure of the Windmills, and a Blanket-tossing

As the knight and squire talked together, they were riding over a part of the country called the Plain of Montiel, where very many windmills stood. There were, indeed, between thirty and forty in all; and the knight had no sooner spied them than he exclaimed delightedly:

"Ha! friend Sancho, Fortune is favouring us better than we could have thought or hoped for. Behold yonder thirty huge giants, towering over the plain. All these I will at once fight and slay, yea, and spoil them of all their riches too. For that is lawful warfare, and doing the world good service also, to rid it of such a monstrous and destructive breed as these giants ever are."

"What giants?" said Sancho, staring about him.

"Why, those straight before you," replied master, "with the long outstretched arms."

"Oh, sir," was Sancho's reply, "those are not giants at all which are standing up yonder, but windmills; and their arms are nothing but the sails, which, when the wind blows, turn round and make the windmills go."

"It is easily seen, Sancho, that you know nothing

about adventures," answered the knight.

"They are most certainly giants, and, if you fear them, stand aside and get to your prayers, whilst I do battle with them."

And, without waiting for more, nor heeding the cries of his squire, who bellowed after him that the wind-mills were windmills indeed and not giants, Don Quixote clapped spurs to Rosinante, and charged full tilt, with couched spear, at the supposed enemy.

As he rushed forward he roared aloud: "Fly not, ye caitiffs! Fly not, ye base poltroons! For here is but one valiant knight who, single-handed, will yet meet and deal with you all!"

Just then a slight wind arose, causing the millsails to begin turning; yet, though he drew ever nearer to them, the knight was unable to see that they were anything but what his fancy would have them. So he galloped on, crying: "Though you move more arms than the giant Briareus, I will make you pay for it!"

Then, calling the name of his lady Dulcinea, he dashed, with outstretched lance, at the nearest wind-mill. The lance struck the sail, which, still continuing to turn, splintered the weapon into a thousand pieces, dragged horse and rider along with it, and finally sent them crashing over on to the plain.

Up rushed Sancho, as fast as his ass could bring him, and found his master unable to rise, so violent was the shock he had received.

"Body o' me!" cried the honest fellow, "did I not tell your worship to mind what you were doing, and not ride a-tilting at foes that were nothing but windmills? And that is what anybody might have seen in the wink of an eye, i' faith, save he who had a windmill in his head!"

"Peace, good friend," replied his master, "for this is but one of the fortunes of war, that are good or ill, as chance ordains. But now I am more than ever certain that the enchanter Friston, who ran off with my library, has, on purpose to vex me and to rob me of the glory of overcoming them, changed these giants into windmills by his evil arts. But they shall all avail nothing against this good sword of mine."

"Heaven grant it may be so, indeed!" said Sancho heartily; and he helped his master to mount once more upon Rosinante, who, poor beast, was much hurt by his fall.

Thus they went forward again, the Don lamenting much for the loss of his lance. But he told Sancho that, after the fashion of one of the heroic knights he had read of, who had also broken his weapon, he would replace his spear with the stout branch of a suitable tree, as soon as he could find one.

"And thou shalt see, good Sancho, what wonders I will do with it, what marvellous feats I will perform," ended the knight.

"Indeed, sir, I am willing to believe all that you say," replied Sancho. "But pray you, now, sir, ride more upright if you can: you are sitting all askew in your saddle, and I am sure that that is all owing to the bruises you got by your late fall.

"Yes, that is so," answered Don Quixote, "and if I do not complain of any pain, it is because no knight-errant is allowed to make an outcry about any wound he may receive—no, not even if his enemies should turn him inside out."

"I have nothing to say to that," said Sancho, "though I hope your honour will tell me whenever anything ails you; but as for me, I am not so tough as the errant knights you talk of; I must cry out when I am hurt—unless this custom of not complaining is to be followed by the squires as well as the knights."

"When you are hurt," said his master, smiling at the simple fellow's words, "you shall cry out as much and as often as you please."

The next day Don Quixote encountered a hot-tempered Biscaine squire, fought with him, and came away from the combat triumphant indeed (for the Biscainer's mule ran away with his rider), but with only half a helmet and half an ear.

The Don was wild with rage and sorrow at the loss of his beloved helmet, vowed to take all sorts of revenges upon the one who had so injured him, and swore that as soon as he could he would find another headpiece by overcoming some chance-met knight on the road, and taking his helmet from him.

"But," objected Sancho, "there are no knights or armed men in these by-roads, my master. There are only carters and carriers and such-like folk, who doubtless never heard of, much less saw, or wore, such a thing as a helmet in all their born days."

"Nay, you are wrong," replied the Don; "I will wager that we shall shortly see as many armed men as came to the famous siege of Albracca."

"Well, since your worship says so, Heaven send them soon, and good success to us, and may your honour speedily win that island you talk of, and then, when you have done so, come what will!" answered the squire.

Later in the day, the knight fell upon some carriers who had hurt Rosinante. They turned upon him, however, beat him and Sancho soundly with their pack-staves, and left the two of them in a very sorry plight.

Don Quixote, in spite of his unhappy condition, called all these disasters but gales of fortune, which should shortly change for them, and blow upon them more favourably. But Sancho declared that just then he was more inclined for sticking plasters than wise or comforting speeches. And, feeling his sore shoulders with many groans and sighs, he observed:

"It is a true saying, indeed, that we are sure of nothing in this life; and there is another thing which I have heard, too, and that is: 'You must eat a peck of salt with your friend before you can know him.' Who would have thought, after the swinging blows that passed between you and yonder Biscainer, that this storm of pack-staves would have fallen upon us too? But if, as you say, sir, all these troubles are but the result of fortune and of chivalry, pray tell me, if you can, whether they are likely to rain upon us often? For it seems to me that if many more alight on our shoulders we shall not be alive to feel them!"

Presently the two came to an inn, which Don Quixote, as was his fashion, declared to be a castle, though Sancho swore it was no more than an inn. The innkeeper came out to receive them; Don Quixote was given a wretched bed in a miserable garret; and the good hostess and her daughter, seeing how bruised and sore he was, set to work to plaster him from head to foot.

The knight and squire spent the night in the inn; and next morning, Don Quixote, feeling much better, was eager to ride out upon his quest once more, for he could not bear to withhold his valiant and chivalrous deeds any longer from a world which he thought stood in such need of them. Poor Sancho was almost too ill to move, but his master saddled his ass for him, helped him upon it, and then rode towards the inn-gate, with his squire behind him.

The folk of the inn gathered round to see him go; and he spoke very graciously to the host, saying how much indebted he was to him, and how, if at any time he should need anyone to avenge a wrong that might be done to him or his, he had only to call upon Don Quixote de la Mancha, that well-known and valiant knight, who would at once see his cause righted, or else do battle for it.

"Sir knight," replied the innkeeper, "I have no need of your worship's avenging arm, for when I am injured by anyone I know how to look after myself, I hope! But I have need of the sum you owe me in payment for the lodging and food that you, your squire, and your two beasts have had here at my inn."

"An inn, is it?" exclaimed the Don. "I made sure it was a castle. But, whatever it be, I know that without a doubt it is against all the laws of knights-errant to pay for any entertainment they may receive: free bed and board are always their due."

"A truce to your knights-errant!" cried the host. "Let me but have that which is lawfully mine, and I care for nothing else!"

"Thou art a blockhead, and a most pitiful fellow besides," answered Don Quixote loftily. And spurring Rosinante forward and brandishing his spear (for he had found a pike in the inn-yard, and taken that for his weapon), he rode out of the gate with never a look behind.

The host seized Sancho, and tried to make him pay the score; but Sancho was as obstinate as his master. If the latter had not paid, neither would he, he declared: the rule which was good for the knight was just as good for the squire. The host scolded and threatened, but Sancho stood firm: if it should cost him his life, said he, he did not mean to pay a single farthing.

Now, as ill luck would have it, this dispute was over-heard by some cloth-workers, needle-makers, and butchers—rough, frolicsome fellows, who were among the guests at the inn. Immediately scenting a chance of mischief, they swept Sancho off his saddle, ran for a blanket, and dumped the squire into the centre of it.

Then, all holding on to the blanket, they got into the

middle of the yard, and began to toss their victim merrily up and down as if he had been a dog at a Shrovetide fair. Sancho was helpless: aloft in the air he flew time after time like an unwieldy feather-bed with wriggling arms and legs attached; then down he would come once more with jolts and bounces that nearly shook him to pieces, and made every bone in his body rattle again.

He roared out threats, scoldings, and entreaties, until the plain rang with his outcries; and his master, riding away from the inn, turned round in wonder at the sound of the uproar, and recognized his squire's voice. Then back he came at a hand-gallop to the inn-yard, but the gate was locked, and all he could do was to rein his steed up close to the high wall, and try to climb over it to Sancho's rescue. This was impossible for him, however, on account of the bruises he had received the day before; he could only just raise himself in his stirrups to look over the wall. The sight of roly-poly Sancho rising and falling in the air like a tossed pancake would have made the knight laugh heartily if he had not been too angry for mirth. His head appeared above the wallstones, from whence he sent down a volley of threats and abuses that would have terrified any folk less careless than the blanket-tossers. They gave not the slightest heed to him, and only made an end of their joke when they had grown heartily weary of it, and could laugh and toss no more.

Then they set Sancho upright on the earth again, lifted him upon his ass, wrapped his cloak around him, threw open the gate, and let him go.

So he dolefully joined his master, very sore in body, but quite satisfied in his mind upon at least one point—that he had not paid a single maravedi to the impudent host. To be sure, he had left his wallet behind in the innkeeper's clutches; but in his confusion and haste he had not missed it.

Still trembling and terribly pale and shaken, he rode beside the knight, who looked down at him and said:

"Now, Sancho, I am perfectly convinced that we are both the unhappy victims of enchantment: that inn was bewitched, those were hobgoblins, and not men, who tossed you, and a spell was laid upon me, also, for the time being, so that I could not even get off my saddle to come to your aid. Be assured, that had I been free to move, I would have made the villains remember the jest as long as they lived, aye, I would, though I have been dubbed a noble knight and they are but lowborn poltroons."

"And so would I i' faith, dubbed or no, if I could, but I could not, shaken to a jelly as I was," answered poor Sancho, "and they were no goblins either, but men like you and me; and I'll wager that it was more stiffness than enchantment that held you from leaping over the fence. And I must say, sir, that if we go after many more adventures such as these, they are like to lead us into worse disadventures, wherein we shall not know our right legs from our left ones. 'Out of the frying-pan, into the fire', as the saying is. To my poor thinking we had far better get back home, seeing that it is reaping-time, and look after our affairs there, and not go running over the world from Cecca to Mecca looking for adventures, and finding nothing but drubbings and cuffs and blanket-tossings for our pains."

5

The Knight of the Sorrowful Figure

As the master and man rode on, a great cloud of dust appeared before them in the distance on the highway, and seemed to be moving slowly in their direction.

"Now, Sancho," exclaimed Don Quixote in delight when he espied it, "now is the time when Fortune's face will smile upon me; to-day is the day when the terrible strength of this right arm of mine shall be proved before all the world, and such feats shall be performed by me this day as shall be written down in letters of gold for the glory and delight of future ages. Seest thou yon cloud of dust, my Sancho? It is caused by the feet of armies—armies of more nations than thou canst count—who are marching in haste towards us."

Sancho looked over his shoulder. "Methinks there are two armies, then," said he, " for here comes just such another cloud of dust behind us."

Another cloud there was, indeed; and at the sight of it the Don rejoiced more than before, being certain that the clouds were raised by two armies which were about to meet and do battle in the middle of the plain where they were. For his mind was full of warlike encounters, challenges, mortal combats, and romantic adventures, and all his thoughts and doings were influ-

enced by his ridiculous passion for chivalry and chivalrous doings.

In reality, the dust was raised by two flocks of sheep,
which were hidden behind the clouds of their own
making, and were travelling that road from different
directions. It was impossible to see them until they
came quite near; but Don Quixote was so sure that
they were no less than armies, that Sancho was quite
ready to believe him.

"What shall we do, sir?" said he, half-scared.

"Do?" replied the valiant Don. "What should we do
but lend the force of our arms to the weaker side?
Now, I must tell you, Sancho, that the army which is
advancing towards us is that of the famous Emperor
Alifanfaron; and the one coming upon us from behind
is the army of his enemy Pentapolin, called Pentapolin
of the Naked Arm, for he ever marches to battle with
his right arm uncovered."

"But why are these two enemies?" demanded Sancho.

"Because," replied his master, "this Alifanfaron, who
is a wicked pagan, wishes to marry the beauteous
daughter of Pentapolin, who refuses to give his child
in marriage to anyone who is not a Christian."

"And very right, too, i' faith!" said Sancho sturdily,
"and so I mean to go and help the good gentleman to
the best of my power."

"So you may, and thus do your duty," replied his
master approvingly. "But, now, pay attention to me,
and I will give you an account of the chief knights of
both armies. See, we will mount yon hillock, from

whence we may have a full view of them all."

The two mounted the rising ground, where they might have seen both flocks of sheep advancing if these had not still been hidden behind the thick dust-clouds.

"Look yonder," cried the Don in a loud voice. And he stretched out his arm, and began to enumerate all the different warriors which he declared were in sight (and indeed, in his crazy fancy no doubt he was quite sure that he actually saw them), describing each one's appearance, arms, and heraldic device with so much detail that one would have said that everything he spoke of was in very truth before his eyes.

Sancho listened, speechless, lost in wonder, looking from side to side now and then for a glimpse of the various knights and furious pagans his master named. But seeing nothing at all but the rapidly advancing dust, he spoke at last.

"Sir, not a knight or a giant or an unbeliever comes before my eyes, for all my looking," said he. "Perhaps it is all enchantment, like the goblins you spoke of but lately."

"What, Sancho!" said the knight, "is it possible that you cannot hear the neighing of steeds, the shrilling of the trumpets, and the rattle of arms and armour?"

"I hear the bleating of sheep and lambs," answered Sancho, "and that is all I can hear." And this was true enough, for the animals were now close beneath them upon the road.

"It is fear, Sancho, which methinks has disturbed your senses, and causes you to see and hear amiss," replied the Don. "But if you are afraid, stand and look on here, whilst with my single arm I will give victory to the righteous cause and that side which I shall favour with my valiant presence and my good sword and lance."

So saying he drove his spurs into Rosinante's flanks and galloped down the hill. Sancho stood still, screeching:

"Hi! Hi! Señor Don Quixote! Master! Master! Come back! Hold, there! Come back, I say! As I live and breathe, they are sheep and not armies which you are going to meet! There is never a knight or a pagan amongst them! Oh, woe upon me, and the day I was born! What mad folly is this! What are you going to do?"

But the knight gave no heed at all to his ravings and warnings. Rushing on like the wind, he charged into the flocks of sheep, scattering them hither and thither and trampling many of them under his horse's feet, whilst he shouted defiance to his enemies and encouragement to his allies.

The angry shepherds shouted too, at this unprovoked and furious onslaught upon their charges, and, unfastening their slings, they began to discharge volleys of stones at Don Quixote. He, however, gave no more heed to the shepherds' stones than he had done to Sancho's calls, but darted amongst the terrified sheep, crying:

"Where art thou, O proud and cruel Alifanfaron? Show thyself to me, and I will engage thee at this moment in single combat, fight thee to the death, and thus punish thee most justly for the wrong thou hast done to the valiant Pentapolin!"

A second later, a large and well-directed stone struck him in the ribs, almost knocking the breath out of his body. Immediately after came another which crashed against his jaw and knocked several of the knight's teeth out. The force of these two blows was so great that he fell from his saddle, quite stunned. The shepherds ran up to look at him where he lay upon the ground white and speechless; and, taking him to be certainly dead, they collected their flocks, gathered up their dead beasts, and hastily fled.

All through this extraordinary encounter Sancho had stood upon the hillock tearing his hair and bemoaning his master's folly. But when the shepherds had vanished, he ran towards the fallen knight, who had now come to himself but could not rise without help.

"Alas, alas!" wailed Sancho when he saw the Don's evil plight, "did I not tell your worship all the time you were a-charging them that the armies were no armies, but innocent sheep?"

"Now you see, as I have often told you, Sancho," said the Don as soon as he could speak, "how my great enemy, the enchanter Friston, can cause things to appear and to vanish again exactly as he wills. For he envied the glory he knew I should gain for my part in this battle, and so, in the malice he bears me, he transformed both those armies into flocks of sheep."

But Sancho, neither comforted nor convinced, stood

beside his faithful ass in a very downcast frame of mind, for besides this present trouble he had just discovered a new misfortune in the loss of his precious wallet.

"Sancho," said his master, laying hold of Rosinante's bridle with one hand, and with the other nursing his wounded jaw tenderly, lest his remaining teeth should drop out, "all these storms that overtake us are but signs, if we would only read them aright, that fortune's weather will clear for us soon. Evil, thou knowest, cannot endure for ever, any more than good. After storm comes the calm, and after hardship, peace and content. Ill times have lasted so long for us that better days cannot possibly be far off now. And again, my good fellow, I cannot see that there is any need for thee to grieve so much for troubles that concern me alone, when thou thyself hast no share in them."

"What, no share?" cried Sancho, lifting his head with an injured air. "Was he that was made to dance in a blanket a few hours ago not my father's son, then? And the wallet I have just missed, was it verily mine, or somebody else's, I should like to know?"

"Is your wallet gone?" said the Don. "That means that we shall have nothing to eat this day. But lift up your heart, nevertheless, good Sancho, and mount Dapple and follow me. For know that Providence careth for all and faileth none, neither the birds of the air, nor the fishes of the deep, nor the beasts of the field, nor man, who is the lord of beasts."

"Methinks your worship makes a better preacher than

a knight-errant," said Sancho with a sniff. "But let us be gone, for mercy's sake, and try to find a shelter for the night. And Fortune grant that it may be in a place where there are neither blankets nor blanket-tossers, nor hobgoblins nor enchanted pagans—for if there be I am sure there will be the mischief and all to pay."

It was some time after this that Sancho, in the course of his chatter, gave his master the title of 'the famous Don Quixote de la Mancha, otherwise called 'the Knight of the Sorrowful Figure''.

"Why do you give me that name, Sancho?" asked the Don.

"Why," replied the squire, "I have been looking at your honour for a long time in this dismal light, and you do, indeed, sir, present the most woeful figure that ever I set eyes on in all my born days. I cannot tell what is the cause of it, unless it is due to the loss of your worship's teeth and all the hardships and skirmishes you have undergone since you left home."

"It is not due to either," replied his master, in no way displeased; "but you must know that the sage who will shortly write the history of my achievements so that all the world may read it, has willed that I should take a surname for myself, after the fashion of all worthy and renowned knights. For one was known as 'The Knight of the Burning Sword', another, as 'The Knight of the Phoenix', a third, as 'The Knight of the Griffin', and so on. And now the sage, as I say, has put it into your head to name me, and into my head to name myself, 'The Knight of the Sorrowful Figure'. And so that I may be ever known by this name wherever I go, I am resolved that upon the first opportunity I will get a most sorrowful figure painted on my shield as my own particular blazon."

"You need not spend either the time or the money on getting that done," was the squire's instant reply. "For your worship has only to show your own face to the world, and then, without sign or shield or blazon to bear you witness, all men will know you as 'Him of the Sorrowful Figure'. Indeed, sir, the lack of food and teeth has made you such a woeful spectacle that the sorrowful figure may very well be spared, to my thinking, at least."

The Don smiled at his squire's jest, and the two rode on until, when darkness had long fallen, they came to a valley, where they dismounted, tethered their beasts, and ate a meal—their breakfast, dinner, and supper all in one—which Sancho supplied. For it must be told that he had, earlier in the evening, rifled the baggage-mule belonging to a company that he and his master had encountered; and the squire considered himself fully justified in claiming and taking another foodwallet, to make up for the loss of his own.

The two ate and drank eagerly; but as there was nothing with which to wash down their meal, the ever-thirsty Sancho suggested that they should move a little farther on to hunt for some fountain or rivulet, which, he said, was almost sure to be found for the searching. So, the one leading Rosinante and the other Dapple, they groped their way slowly forward through the black night, scarcely seeing a foot before them.

Presently they heard with delight the roar of a waterfall, but as they stopped to make sure from which direction the sound came, another sound fell upon their ears, and set poor Sancho all atremble. It was a succession of heavy blows, delivered regularly and unceasingly and with a mighty clamour, mingled with a dragging and rattling of heavy chains—a noise that might well have struck terror into any heart less fearless than that of the bold Don. We have said that the night was very dark, and now it seemed even darker by reason of some tall trees into whose shade they had strayed, and whose weird rustling, mixed with the moan of the wind, the rushing of the waters, the hammering blows and the clanking of the mysterious chains, added to the horror of their present plight and uncertain position.

But our valiant knight, nothing daunted by all this, leaped upon Rosinante's saddle, braced his shield, brandished his spear, and thus addressed his quaking squire:

"Know, friend Sancho, that I was born in this iron age to revive the age of gold. I am he for whom the most desperate adventures, the most frightful dangers, and the most glorious achievements have been reserved. To my name, in future ages, all your Olivers, your Knights of the Sun, and your war-like Belianises, will be as nothing, for my unheard-of deeds will outdo them all. Observe, my good squire, the darkness and desolation that surround us; hear the noise of the waters, which seem to fall from the very mountains of the moon, and the strange and horrible clanging that comes we know not whence. All this, I say, would be enough to affright the heart of Mars himself, yet I, Don Quixote de la Mancha, quail not before it. Nay, upon the contrary, that which I cannot see but can only too plainly hear, does but rouse me to further endeavours and sets me aflame to undertake this new and unknown adventure. Gird up Rosinante well and truly, then, and now Heaven be with you. Stay here for me three days, and if I return not, go back to our village and from thence take your ways to Toboso, where you may tell my lady Dulcinea that I died in an adventure of such worthiness as might indeed entitle me to be termed her faithful and adoring knight."

At the Don's words poor Sancho began to blubber noisily. "Alas, sir," he said, "where is the need for all this pother, and this talk of dying in adventures? Why need you meddle with such things at all? The night is black enough, I am sure: who is to see us if we sneak away and get far from here before worse trouble befalls us, even though we have to go waterless for three days or more? The good priest of our village, whom your worship knows, has many a time preached that those who seek danger perish in it. Why in the world do you want to tempt Providence by seeking for trouble, then? Nay, if all these arguments of mine will not move you, bethink yourself of me, your poor squire, sir. Here I am, and if you take it into your head to leave me, I shall be ready, out of sheer fright, to give up my soul to whoever will take it. Consider, sir; I left

my home and my wife and children to follow your
honour, thinking I should profit and not lose by so
doing.

But 'Covetousness bursts the bag' is a saying that is
like to prove true enough in my case; for it seems that
just as I was hoping to make a good thing or this
knight-erranting, and expecting to have that unlucky
island which you promised me for my pains, your
knightship goes off and abandons me in this dreadful
unholy place far from the good daylight and the cheerful haunts of men. At least, sir, if you must undertake
this misventure, wait until daybreak. It cannot be more
than three hours off now, for the muzzle of the Great
Bear is directly above our heads, and that makes mid-
night in the line of my left arm."

"How can you see either muzzle or line, Sancho,"
said the Don, "when the night is dark as pitch, and not
a star shines in the sky?"

"That's true, your worship," replied the squire, in no
way abashed, "but fear has many eyes, and sees a
score of things that are even under the earth, let alone
in the heavens. But, in any case, I am sure that it
cannot be far off daybreak."

But neither arguments nor entreaties could hold the
knight. He only bade Sancho hold his tongue and buckle
up Rosinante's girths. Then the squire, finding his master so obstinate, and equally determined upon his side
that the Don should not go and leave him, did as he
was told, but at the same time slyly slipped off his
ass's halter and with it securely tied the horse's hind

legs. Thus, when Don Quixote spurred Rosinante to go forward, he could only move in short, bucking jumps.

"Ah, sir," said Sancho, finding how this trick answered, "you see how Heaven has been kind to my prayers and tears, and so hindered Rosinante from stirring from this place; and if you urge him forward now, you will only 'kick against the pricks' as folk say."

The Don fumed and raged, and spurred his steed again, but discovering that all was in vain, for all the attacks on his horse's flanks had not the least effect upon the poor beast's legs, he gave up the attempt until day should dawn.

So throughout the long night they waited where they were; and Sancho told a rambling tale of romance to his master, to pass the time, for neither of them could sleep, so terrifying were the darkness and the ceaseless din in their ears.

When the dawn came at last, they found they were in a gloomy grove of tall chestnut trees, which hid from sight the cause of the resounding blows that still continued. By this time Sancho had untied Rosinante as gently and cautiously as he had tied him. The steed, finding himself free, began to stir thankfully, and as his master felt him move he took it for a good omen, once more bade farewell to his squire, repeated his commands and his message to his lady, and spurred forward.

Sancho began to weep afresh, but now he determined that, however much his master might wish to leave him, he would on no account leave his master. He therefore followed the knight on foot, leading Dapple by the halter. The two men passed through the grove towards the sound of the falling waters and the great blows, and came out at last in a little green meadow below some huge rocks down which a cascade of water tumbled, foaming and crashing. Several half-ruined huts stood at the foot of the rocks, and from these huts the sound of the blows came with redoubled violence. Poor Rosinante started and trembled, but his rider soothed him, and went forward at a slow pace with his lance couched and behind him his timorous squire who peeped fearfully between Rosinante's legs every moment as he advanced.

A hundred yards farther on, a turn round a sharp projecting rock brought them in full view of the cause of the mysterious and dreadful sound that all night long had held them in such suspense and fear. It was neither more nor less than half a dozen huge fulling-mill hammers, which, in their work of beating cloth night and day, had made the continuous, thundering blows which our adventurers had heard.

Don Quixote stared agape at the sight, struck dumb with amazement and confusion. Sancho, watching him, saw his head sink upon his breast in embarrassment; then the knight glanced up again, and caught his squire's mocking eyes. They were brimming over with merriment, and the other, as he looked at him, could not help breaking into laughter at the absurdity of the whole thing.

The man took his cue from his master, and, almost doubling himself in two, roared aloud in his mirth, holding his sides. Again and again he broke into fresh fits of laughter, until the Don quite lost patience. But when Sancho waggishly began in his master's very voice: "Know, friend Sancho, that I was born in this iron age to revive the age of gold. I am he for whom the most desperate adventures, the most frightful dangers, and the most glorious achievements have been reserved," the knight's temper got the better of him. Raising his lance, he brought it down upon his pert follower's shoulders with such force that, had the blow landed on Sancho's head instead, it would have relieved the master of any payment of wages to his man.

But Sancho dodged, and then cried aloud: "Body o' me, sir, calm yourself! I was but jesting with your worship, after all."

"Though you may jest, fellow, I do not," replied Don Quixote loftily. "And suppose," he went on, "that these mill-hammers had in truth been some desperate adventure, did I not go forward with just as great a courage, just as stout a heart, as if they had been so, though I knew not what they were? Suppose the fulling-mills were changed into six huge giants before our eyes, and suppose they were to set upon me one by one—why, then, if I did not meet them all, and lay every one of them by the heels, you might make of me what jest you would."

"Indeed, sir," answered Sancho humbly, "I confess that I have been a little too merry at your honour's expense. But when all is said, my master, was it not a matter for laughter, and for telling over a second time—the tremendous fear we were in (at least, that I was in, I ought rather to say), and all for a set of fulling-mill hammers?"

"It may have been," replied the Don, "but such experiences are better kept to ourselves than told again; for all folk, you know, Sancho, are not prudent enough to take things by the right handle, as it were."

"Faith!" was Sancho's reply, "I think your worship took your lance by the wrong handle but now, when you aimed it at my head and brought it down upon my shoulders, thanks to my own nimbleness in ducking aside! But that may well pass—'twill all come out in the washing, as the saying is; for there is a right good proverb which tells us that: 'He loves thee well who makes thee weep.' And, moreover, 'tis the custom among gentry, after they have given their servants a hard word or so, to make up for it by the present of a cast-off jerkin or an old pair of hose. But what the servants of knights-errant are apt to get after a drubbing I know not, unless it may be an island or a kingdom, or some such thing."

"Perhaps it may be," replied Don Quixote, "and there is no reason why what you wish may not come to pass. So let us forget and forgive, Sancho; for a man has not always the power to control his first hasty actions. And now, let me warn you not to make so free with me, your master, in the future, and to set a curb upon your too-freely wagging tongue. For in all the books of chivalry that ever I read, I never discovered that any squire chattered so much to his master as you do to yours."

6

How the Don took Mambrino's Helmet, and went to the Sable Mountain

After a little while the two struck the highroad again, and presently the knight saw, advancing towards them, a mounted traveller, who wore on his head something which glittered like gold.

Don Quixote, at the sight of the stranger, turned to his squire.

"Now I am persuaded of the truth of all proverbs, Sancho," said he, "for every one is a saying full of wisdom drawn from actual experience. Take as an instance the one which tells us that: 'There is never one door shuts but another opens.' For last night Fortune shut the door upon us indeed in the affair of the fulling-mills, thereby deceiving us most unfortunately; but today she opens another to us that promises us an adventure more profitable and sure. And if I fail in this one the fault is mine, for now there is neither the darkness of the night nor my own ignorance of fulling-mills to lead me astray. I tell you this because here advancing towards us comes one, if I am not mistaken, who is wearing the helmet of Mambrino, and you cannot have forgotten the vow I took concerning that."

Now Mambrino was a king of the Saracens, who, in one of the Don's beloved stories of romance, was plundered of his helmet by a knight named Reynaldos de Montalvan. It will be remembered that, after his own helmet was broken, our valiant Don vowed to follow such a knightly example in order to provide himself with another, upon the first opportunity he should have. Therefore, seeing the advancing rider with the glittering headpiece, he was now quite certain that his chance of gaining another helmet was come at last.

"I would advise your honour to have a care what you say, and a greater care what you do," said the cautious Sancho. "I have no mind, and neither have you, I should hope, sir, for anymore fulling-mills to mash and pound our wits to powder."

"Silly fellow!" replied his master, "what has a helmet got to do with fulling-mills, pray?"

"Nay, I know not," answered the squire, "but if I were allowed to speak as freely as I was wont to do before your worship rebuked me for chattering, perhaps my words would prove to you that you are mistaken."

"How, mistaken!" said the Don scornfully. "Tell me, can you not see yon knight pricking tow-ards us on a dapple-grey steed, and wearing upon his head a helmet of gold?"

"All I see," quoth Sancho, "is a man coming our way mounted upon a grey ass like my Dapple, and carrying some glittering thing on his head."

"Well, that is Mambrino's helmet," was the knight's impatient reply. "Stand out of the way, and you shall shortly see me deal with him neatly and briefly, and the helmet I have vowed to win shall be mine indeed."

"Oh, I will keep out of the way smartly enough," answered Sancho, "but I pray Heaven that it may not prove another fulling-mill adventure, that's all."

"Not another word of fulling-mills!" cried the irritated knight, "or by my head, I will mill thee!"

The real truth of the matter was this, however. In their immediate neighbourhood were two villages, one small and the other fairly large. The smaller one boasted neither barber's shop nor barber; the other had both, and thus one barber served for the two villages, riding from one to the other whenever his services were called for. On this particular day he was going to the little village to perform some necessary shaving and bloodletting, and, according to his custom, was taking his brass basin with him. But as he rode along the way, rain began to fall heavily; the barber, who had on a new hat which he had no mind to spoil, clapped his basin over it to preserve it; and the basin, being freshly polished, glittered like gold a great distance off. He rode upon a grey ass, as Sancho had said; but to the romance-stuffed mind of the Don he appeared as nothing less than a golden-helmeted knight upon a grey charger.

Don Quixote stopped for neither explanations nor arguments, even had any been demanded or offered. Couching his lance, and setting Rosinante at a lumbering gallop, he charged the unlucky barber, shouting as he came on:

"Defend thyself, thou recreant, or render up to me

that which is my due!"

When he saw this terrible figure bearing down upon him with outstretched lance directed right at his heart, the barber, speechless with fright, tumbled headlong from his saddle to avoid the coming blow. No sooner did he feel the ground beneath him than he got to his feet as nimbly as a monkey, and, never stopping to pick up his fallen basin or to look behind him once, set off in frantic flight over the plain, and was soon out of sight.

The Don, quite satisfied at this result of his charge, wheeled round and rode back to his open-mouthed squire, whom he ordered to pick up the prize that the barber had left in the dust.

The man did as he was bidden, and held up the basin admiringly. "Upon my word!" said he, "'tis a special one, by the looks of it, and as well worth a piece-of-eight as a farthing."

The knight took it from his hand, and immediately put it upon his own head, twisting it round to find the visor. Not being able to discover it, he observed gravely that "the pagan for whom it was first fashioned must have owned a mighty large head; and even as the helmet was, one half of it was missing."

At the word helmet Sancho began to snigger, but checked himself when he found his master's eye upon him. "Why do you laugh, sirrah?" demanded Don Quixote.

"I laugh to think what a great skull that pagan must have had, to wear this helmet, which is for all the world like a barber's basin," replied Sancho demurely.

"I will tell you how it is, good friend," said the knight confidently. "This famous enchanted headpiece has assuredly, at some time or other, fallen by chance into the hands of someone who knew not what it was, nor knew its true value. But, seeing it to be of purest gold, that person has melted it down, sold one half, and out of the other he has made this, which does look like a barber's basin indeed, as you say. But that is no matter to me; let it seem what it may, I know what it really is, and so am content. For I will have it rightly made, with a visor, in the next town where we find an armourer, and when it is properly fashioned it will have no equal in all the world. Meanwhile, I will even wear it as it is."

Some little time after this adventure the knight and squire encountered another which proved to be not so profitable and far more unpleasant. For they met a string of chained and manacled prisoners who, guarded by armed men, were on their way to the coast to serve as galley-slaves, this being their punishment for the various crimes they had committed. Don Quixote stopped the guards, questioned the prisoners, and then, being convinced that it was his duty, as a knight-errant, to succour all the needy and distressed, requested the guards to set the captives free. This, needless to say, they stoutly refused to do, whereat the Don flew into a passion and attacked them. He might have had the worst of the encounter had not the prisoners themselves, seeing their guards so occupied, broken the

chain which bound them and turned upon their perse-
cutors, sending them, in the end, far and wide in flight
across the plain.

The slaves then gathered about Don Quixote, whom
they looked upon as their rescuer, and asked him what
his pleasure might be. But when they were told that he
expected them all to journey to Toboso to pay homage
to the lady of his heart, the beauteous Dulcinea, and
render her a true account of her knight's chivalrous
and valiant deed, the rogues were not so ready to obey
him. The Don, enraged, vowed that they should: the
chief spokesman among them swore that they would
not. Words rose high; but at length the prisoners, taking matters into their own hands, began to stone Don
Quixote as hard as they could, until he was brought to
the earth, when the spokesman, throwing himself upon
him, took off his heavy brass helmet and thumped him
soundly upon the shoulders with it. The fellows then
stripped the knight and squire of their jackets and
cloaks, and, leaving them to make what shift they could,
took to their heels and fled, fearing that the Holy Brotherhood, as the body of police in Spain was called at
that time, might find them out and bring them back to
justice.

It was this very fear of the Brotherhood which urged
Sancho, as soon as he could get his master's consent,
to turn their beasts' heads towards the heights called
the Sierra Morena range. Here, in the heart of what
was known as the Sable Mountain, amongst the savage, rocky fastnesses of that wild region, the squire

thought they would do well to hide themselves for a few days from the prying eyes of the law, which he was very well aware they had insulted by meddling with prisoners of the state.

Into the desolations of the Sable Mountain, then, they entered presently, Sancho congratulating himself that their late assailants had overlooked his wallet in plundering him and his master of their clothes. They spent the night among the rocks; but while they slept poor Dapple was stolen away from his fond master by the ringleader of the escaped prisoners who had also taken refuge in the Sable Mountain.

Sancho, waking next morning and immediately missing his ass, set up a most doleful lamentation.

"Alas, alas, dear child of my heart!" he wailed, "thou who wast born under my roof, the joy of my children, the pleasure of my wife, the envy of my neighbours, the bearer of my burdens, the very half of my maintenance—for thou wast the means of earning me six-and-twenty maravedis daily, and with this I supported half my family! Alas, alas! where art thou gone, my Dapple?"

His continued cries awoke his master, who, learning the cause of them, consoled him as well as he could, promising, at the same time, to let him have three asses' colts out of the five which he had at home. Sancho was much cheered at this, and thanked the Don gratefully for his generosity.

Don Quixote was delighted to find himself in that wild mountain country; for it was in such places, he thought, where the most marvellous adventures were most likely to be encountered. He called to mind all the knights-errant he had ever read about, who had retired to remote and solitary places of the earth and found strange happenings and undertaken stranger enterprises therein. And in his own mind he resolved forthwith to follow their example as closely as he could.

"Sancho," said he, when after wandering for some time they had come to a very lonely and rocky part of the mountains, "I have a mind to remain here for a while, in order to perform a notable exploit that shall be the wonder of all ages to come. for you must know, that as the renowned Amadis de Gaul retired to that solitary place called the Poor Rock, and there performed a hard and lengthy penance because he was scorned by his lady Oriana, so do I intend to do as he did; and thus by imitating the flower of knighthood I shall arrive myself at the very perfection of chivalry."

"But what is it that your honour means to do?" asked Sancho, only half understanding him.

"To run clean mad for grief," was the Don's astonishing answer, "even as those gallant knights of old, Amadis and Orlando, did, we are told, when they were disdained by the ladies of their hearts. To weep and lament and beat my breast, to dash my head against the flinty rocks and mingle my tears with the waters of the mountain springs, to wander ill-clothed and fasting amongst the crags and morasses, and to rend the heavens with my pitiable wailings. All this I mean to do; therefore hinder me not, but waste no more time and

let me get to this new and admirable undertaking as
fast as I may."

"But what does your worship want to run mad for?"
cried Sancho, staring. "What lady has scorned you? Or
has your sweetheart Madam Dulcinea disdained you
and cast you off for another?"

"These eyes have not beheld my honoured lady
Dulcinea for many a weary day," replied the Don. "I
know not how her feelings may have changed towards
me, for thou knowest that the poet says: 'Every ill is
felt and feared by the absent.' But that is all one—mad
I am, and mad I will be, until thou shalt return to me
here with an answer from my lady Dulcinea to the
letter which I now command thee to bear to her. And
by means of this letter she shall know all that her loyal
champion endures for her sake, and I shall know by
her reply whether my suffering faithfulness is in vain
or no. For if she returns a gracious answer and bids me
leave off the penance that I am about to undergo on
her account, I will be mad no longer. But if she dis-
dains my entreaties, then I shall take leave of my senses
in very truth."

The two presently came to the foot of a steep and
darkly-frowning rock which reared itself far above the
other crags that surrounded it. A pleasant stretch of
greensward lay before it, shaded by some great forest
trees and watered by a clear mountain stream; and
upon beholding the scene our Knight of the Sorrowful
Figure immediately decided that this should be the place
of his penance. He made a high-flown speech to the

rocks and trees and waters, bidding them behold the pain that his tortured heart endured. And he called upon his lady Dulcinea, the light of his eyes, the star of his being, to relent from her cruelty and look with pity upon him and the state to which her absence and indifference had reduced him.

"I beseech you, sir," said Sancho, "When you get to the gnashing and dashing part of this punishment of yours, have a care where and how you knock yourself about. For to my thinking, if such bangs are indeed necessary, as your honour seems to think (though I understand they are no more than a sham), why, then, you might content yourself with knocking yourself against something soft, whilst you are about it, and let the trees and rocks alone. And trust me to let Madam Dulcinea know that you ran your head against a rock that is harder than a diamond! But now, sir, write the letter, and give me leave to set off with it; for I long to have your worship out of this kettle of fish, once and for all."

The letter was written accordingly, and filled with high-sounding phrases of adoration, and declarations of grief at the fair one's cruelty, together with entreaties that she would bestow her favour upon the desperate writer, and so release him from his penance. It was signed: "Thine till death, The Knight of the Sorrowful Figure"; and this extraordinary letter Sancho undertook to deliver to the country maiden at Toboso, and at the same time to carry to Don Quixote's niece a note for the ass-colts promised by the knight to his squire.

Rosinante was saddled, therefore, at once, and Sancho mounted him and rode away, his last view of his master being the spectacle of Don Quixote de la Mancha, half-dressed, cutting a series of wild and absurd capers at the foot of the rock, by way of beginning his penance.

7

How Don Quixote went Home

Sancho, when he got out of the regions of the Sable Mountain, and on to the high-road, turned Rosinante's head towards Toboso; and after riding all that day, came early upon the day thazt followed to the inn where he and his master had spent one night, and where the unlucky blanket-tossing had taken place.

At first the squire decided that he would avoid the house; but hunger and the need of rest nearly overcame his resolution. He was just doubting whether he would enter the inn or no, when two persons came out of it and approached him. They knew him almost immediately, and he them, for they were no others than his master's friends, the priest and barber of his own village.

They inquired, of course, after the Don at once; and Sancho gave them an account of the adventures that had befallen the two since they left home, of the knight's present strange freak, and of how he himself was carrying a letter to the damsel at Toboso, whom her admirer called the lady Dulcinea. They then asked to see the letter; but Sancho, when he felt in his pocket for it, discovered to his dismay that it was not there, and that his master's order for the colts was likewise missing. The poor fellow tore his beard and hair, and rent the air with lamentations, making sure that he had lost the papers; but in reality he had never carried them away from the Sable Mountain, for the Don had forgotten, at the last moment, to give them to him.

The priest comforted him for the loss of the order, telling him that, as soon as he met the Don, he would remind him to renew it for his squire's sake. Then the barber asked him whether he could remember the letter; and Sancho, after shifting from one foot to the other, scratching his head, and biting his nails for some time, declared that: "It began: 'High and subterrane lady'"

"Not subterrane, but rather sovereign lady, Sancho," corrected the barber.

"Yes, sovereign lady," went on Sancho, "and it ended: 'Thine till death, The Knight of the Sorrowful Figure', and there was a score of sighs, and hearts, and darts, and bewailings in between. And if the lady Dulcinea sends back a kindly answer to this message (which would indeed melt the heart of a stone), my master will straightway cease to be mad for grief, and will up and ride out again like the hero that he is, and set forth to conquer some kingdom or other, and reign in it as emperor, and thereby enrich his poor squire."

The priest and the barber marvelled at the ridiculous folly of master and man; but they decided that Don Quixote should be brought from the Sable Mountain as speedily as might be, and, if possible, they would persuade him to give up his penance and return quietly to his own home. Therefore, after Sancho had rested and fed outside the inn, all three set off for the place where the squire had left his master.

It was first of all their idea that Sancho should tell the Don that the lady Dulcinea, having the letter delivered to her, and being unable to read or write herself, had sent a message by the squire that the knight should go to her at once upon a matter of the utmost importance. If this plan did not answer, the barber said, he himself would put on woman's dress and go before Don Quixote, acting the part of a distressed damsel who besought his aid in avenging her for the insults she had suffered at the hands of a discourteous knight.

They were saved this trouble, however; for before they reached the region where the Don was performing his penance, they fell in with some company amongst whom was a lady, who, when she heard all the story of Don Quixote and his whim, offered at once to play the distressed damsel, to oblige them.

Sancho had meanwhile gone on before them, and found his master still below the rock, worn and enfeebled by his penance, and half starved as well. The lady Dulcinea's supposed request had no effect upon him; he was determined not to appear before her until he had performed some heroic deed that should be worthy of her, he declared. Sancho gloomily returned with his tale to the priest and barber and the rest of the company. The priest, however, comforted him by telling him that his master should be very soon brought away from that place, whether he liked it or not.

"You see this beautiful lady, Sancho," said he. "She

is called the Princess Micomicona, heiress of the kingdom of Micomicon, and she comes to beg a great boon of your master—to request him to overthrow, by his strength and renowned prowess, a wicked giant who has invaded and seized her kingdom."

"That he may very well do," quoth Sancho, "if he meets him—that is, unless the giant is a goblin, for my master has no power over goblins and such-like folk. And in my opinion 'twould be an excellent thing," added he, lowering his voice so that none but the priest could hear, "if you could persuade his worship, when he has slain the giant and delivered the princess, to marry her at once, and so come to reign over the kingdom as an emperor should do, and as he has declared he would do, too, as soon as he could find a kingdom to reign over."

The priest assured him that he would do all in his power to advise the Don well, being secretly astonished and amused, meanwhile, at the simple mind of the man who could believe such a tale and take for sober truth all the absurdities with which the master had filled his brain.

The company set out for Don Quixote's retreat, and the priest followed them on foot, meaning to meet them later on. When they came in sight of the knight lamenting below his rock, the lady rode forward, dismounted from her palfrey, and threw herself at his feet, declaring that she would never rise until he had granted her the boon she had come to crave. The Don gallantly protested, but the lady persisted; and at length he said: "Rise, O beauteous and worthy lady, for I herewith grant you the boon, provided that in bestowing it I may be called upon to do nothing that shall disgrace my king, my country, or her who is the ruler of my heart."

"What I ask will not shame any of these"—the lady was beginning, when Sancho struck in:

"Your worship may take my word that it will be quite safe to do as madam desires. 'Tis nothing—nothing at all but to kill a clumsy lubber of a giant. And the lady is the great Princess Micomicona, the reigning queen of Micomicon in Ethiopia—think of that!"

"'Tis no matter to me who she may be," replied the Don solemnly, "for to any poor female in distress I will do my duty, in accordance with the rules of the noble profession of knighthood."

The lady then put her pretended case before him, begging him to promise her that he would allow her to lead him whithersoever she would, and also that he would engage in no other adventure until he had avenged her cause.

The Don, much moved, promised all that she asked. He ordered Sancho to prepare Rosinante and to help him on with his armour immediately; and crying: "Let us ride forth at once to the succour of this most distressed and unhappy lady!" he presently led the way out of the wilderness, with the others behind him.

Upon the plain at the mountain foot they were met by the priest, who greeted Don Quixote with many shows of surprise, and much delight, the Don being no less pleased, upon his part, at the meeting.

As the company went forward, the knight asked the supposed princess to lead the way in whatever direction she thought best; whereat the priest said politely and meaningly: "I presume, madam, that you will make your way towards the kingdom of Micomicon?"

The lady, well schooled in the part she was to play, replied that she certainly meant to go thither, and the priest answered immediately: "Then our road lies straight through my own village in La Mancha, whence you must take a direct route to Carthagena, and there embark for your kingdom." Such were their wily but most kindly-meant plans for carrying the unsuspecting knight back to his own home.

Very soon, in the distance on the road before them, appeared a man like a gipsy, riding upon an ass. Sancho, with his eyes almost starting from his head, knew both man and beast at once, for they were no others than the evil-hearted ringleader of the galley-slaves whom Don Quixote had freed, and Sancho's own beloved Dapple.

"Ha, rogue!" bawled the squire on the instant, "get you gone, you thief, you villain, you stealer of honest men's goods, and leave me my darling, my joy, my Dapple, the delight of my heart!"

The robber, scared at the words and the sight of the company, tumbled off the ass in a frantic hurry, and, leaving him standing, took to his heels and fled, never stopping until he was far out of sight.

Then Sancho, shouting in his delight, rushed up to

Dapple and embraced and kissed him, crying: "How art thou, my sweetheart, my dearest Dapple? How hast thou fared, away from thine own master this long while?" The good creature stood patiently to be kissed and petted and talked to like a human being; and Sancho, nearly beside himself with joy, received the congratulations of all the company upon the return of his treasure.

After this, his master drew Sancho aside, and asked him a thousand questions concerning the fair Dulcinea; where, how, and when he found her, what she had said, what she was doing, and how she received his letter. Sancho confessed that he had gone without the letter, but declared he had remembered it so well that he had got a parish clerk to write it down at his dictation, and this message he had delivered to Dulcinea. Then, upon the knight's further questioning, he made up a tale of how he had found the lady winnowing wheat in her backyard, of how he had given her a pitiful account of his master's penance, and delivered his letter to her, and how she sent back a message that she desired above all things to see her faithful knight. And with this pretty story Don Quixote was obliged to be satisfied.

Once more they came to the inn of Sancho's blanket-tossing adventure, where they supped all together, the worn-out knight retiring long before the others, to seek some sleep in the garret-chamber he had occupied before.

But as the folk of the inn were all sitting with their

guests after supper, Sancho, in a most excited state, came rushing out of his master's room.

"Help, sirs! Oh, help! help! for mercy's sake! Or rather, come and see, come and see! My valorous master is at this very moment up to the ears in the most terrible combat you ever beheld! May the mischief take me, if he has not even now given that craven-hearted mountain of a giant, the oppressor of the Princess Micomicona, such a thwack that he has severed his head from his shoulders as if it had been a turnip! Sure, the villain's blood is flooding the chamber floor, and there is his head rolled aside, as big as a wine-skin!"

The whole company rushed into the knight's room, and there beheld Don Quixote de la Mancha, out of his bed and upon his feet and laying about him with a will, sword in hand, yet fast asleep the whole time. For he had been dreaming that he was encountering the giant, so full was his mind of the adventure which he supposed he was to undertake. Thus, imagining that he was felling his enemy, he had struck in his sleep at a number of great wine-skins which were standing in the room, slashing at them with his weapon, cutting them half to pieces, and sending rivers of crimson wine all over the floor.

A tremendous uproar followed. The innkeeper stormed and threatened at the loss of all his good wine; the barber poured a bucketful of cold water over the knight, to awaken him; the priest tried to pacify the innkeeper, and Sancho, hunting all about for the head of the giant and not finding it, roared aloud that the whole place was enchanted, of a truth, as he had suspected ever since he had visited it before.

At length some kind of order was restored. The knight, now awake, making sure that his undertaking was at last accomplished, knelt down and said: "Beauteous and renowned lady, from this day you may live in all peace and security, unharmed by any enemy; and by this exploit I am released from the promise I made to you." Some of the company coaxed him into bed once more, and left him to sleep until the morning. Then the priest promised the wrathful host that he should have full amends for the loss of his wine and for any other damage that had been done; and after this the company retired, to spend the rest of the evening in quietness.

More travellers came to the inn upon the two days that followed; and Don Quixote got into several more scrapes, and got out of them again, more by good luck than his own good management; whilst Sancho declared that the unlucky house was certainly bewitched, for there was no spending a single peaceable hour in it.

Now the priest and Master Nicholas the barber were very anxious to get the Don home without troubling the lady (who had met some friends of hers at the inn) to ride so far out of her way as the knight's village. They therefore devised a new plan of their own.

Don Quixote, wearied out with his late exertions, was resting on his bed, and safely out of the way, when a man with a wagon and a team of oxen came up to the inn. No sooner had Master Nicholas and the priest spied him than they made a bargain with him for the hire of his wagon and his beasts. They then made a great cage of poles, large enough to contain a man; and when this was finished and ready, a number of the company, including the priest and the barber, went up to the Don's chamber. At the priest's direction they had all disguised themselves in great cloaks and hideous masks; and they now proceeded, in dead silence, to bind Don Quixote hand and foot so that he was not able to stir. When the astounded knight awakened, he found himself being tied, and then he was borne towards the cage by a number of frightful-looking creatures the like of which he had never beheld before. He was too much surprised to utter a word; but immediately concluded that the castle (as he had ever imagined the inn) was bewitched, and that the awful shapes about him were goblins. And without doubt, he thought, he himself had been enchanted too, since he was helpless as a log and unable to move a limb.

Into the cage his weird captors hoisted him, nailing up the bars so tightly that there was no possibility of escape. They then lifted it upon their shoulders, and were bearing it out of the room when a mysterious voice was suddenly heard, speaking in as deep and dreadful tones as the barber could command.

"O Knight of the Sorrowful Figure," it said, "be not grieved that thou art thus taken captive and borne away. Such imprisonment is necessary that thou mayst the more speedily accomplish the heroic and renowned adventure in which thou art so honourably engaged. And thou, O most faithful and obedient squire who ever wore belt on body or beard on chin, be not cast down to behold thy valorous master treated thus. Thou shalt see thyself, when the time is ripe, in high estate and in possession of thy full wages. Follow thy noble lord, then, whithersoever he is taken, which is to a place where both thou and he may rest secure and content. Because I am now permitted to say no more, fare you well. I go back to the place where I belong."

This astonishing prophecy consoled Don Quixote wonderfully, and, though still marvelling at the whole mysterious affair, he was now somewhat more willing to submit to his strange fate. The cloaked figures carried the cage outside to the wagon, Rosinante and Dapple were saddled, and the procession set forth.

The wagon, drawn by its team of oxen and guided by the wagoner, went first, bearing the cage with its bound and patient captive, and guarded by some troopers of the Holy Brotherhood who had been engaged by the priest. Then came Sancho mounted upon Dapple, and leading Rosinante who carried the knight's buckler and basin-helmet, one on either side of his saddle. After these rode Master Nicholas and the priest, still wearing their cloaks and masks, bringing up the rear of the cavalcade, silent and solemn, and keeping their horses at a slow walk to suit the creeping pace of the oxen.

Thus, with many a halt, and after encountering more

adventures than we have space to set down here, the
party travelled for five or six days; and at length, one
Sunday noontide, entered Don Quixote's village. The
streets were filled with gossiping loungers; and when
the wagon and its burden passed through the market-
place, the folk thronged and jostled to catch a glimpse
of the person in the cage. When he was discovered to
be no other than their own neighbour, every man and
woman was agape with astonishment; and an urchin
ran off to tell the knight's niece and housekeeper that
the master of the house had come home, feeble and
wretched-looking, borne on a truss of straw in an ox-
wagon.

At this news the two women set up a woeful outcry;
but at last they got him into the house and into bed,
where he lay quietly, looking at them both wonderingly,
but recognizing neither of them, so greatly had his
recent hardships and adventures affected his mind and
body.

The priest bade them care for him well, and watch
over him lest he should escape them to go off adven-
turing again as soon as he was better. For this was
what the good man feared most of all, and what, indeed, actually came to pass in the course of time.

PART 2

1

The Enchantment of Dulcinea

For about a month after Don Quixote was brought home his two friends, the priest and Master Nicholas, did not visit him, for they wished to give him time to recover in both mind and body from his late adventures. Above all things the priest wished the poor gentleman's frenzy concerning knight-errantry to vanish altogether, if possible; and he therefore would not see him, lest the sight of his friends should awaken the knight's remembrance of his former misfortunes.

The friends inquired about his health, however, every day; and at length, getting such good reports from the Don's niece and housekeeper, they one day paid him a visit. He greeted them with great pleasure, and began to talk to them upon all sorts of subjects with much sense and wisdom; but presently his conversation turned to the topic of knight-errantry, and they were soon able to discover that, upon this subject, and this subject only, his wits were as far astray as they had ever been.

"Mark my words, neighbour," said the priest to Master Nicholas as they left him, "our friend will be off again upon another ramble ere he is many weeks older."

Another friend was introduced to Don Quixote about this time. This was a young scholar named Samson

Carrasco, who had just taken the degree of bachelor of arts at the University of Salamanca. He was a droll waggish spark, with a great love of all kinds of fun and of practical joking. In conversations with Don Quixote he praised the knight up to the skies, declaring that all Spain, not to mention other countries, was by this time ringing with the fame of his exploits. Sancho Panza listened to these long talks, and declared himself ready to follow his master forth again, whenever it should please him.

"Though," added he, "it must be known that I set out with no intention of doing battle with any myself—not I. I will fetch and carry for his worship as good as any spaniel; but as for thumps and thwacks, why, I leave those to him. For I do not set up to be valiant; I only hope for the fame of being considered the most faithful and trusty squire that ever rode after a knight-errant. And if my master, remembering my good services and his good promises, has a mind to give me that island which he says he is bound to light upon, why, then, many thanks to him for it. But if it comes not in my way I have no doubt I may well make shift without it, and live and die plain Sancho Panza, and let the governorship alone. Yet, at the same time, if it happens to be there for the taking, I'll not be so great a fool as to say nay to it. 'When a heifer is given thee, make haste with the halter,' is a good saying; and another one is: 'When good fortune knocks at the door, be sure to let her in.'"

Don Quixote told Carrasco that it was his intention

to ride forth shortly upon another quest and asked his advice about the beginning of his journey. The bachelor then let him know that a great military tournament, in honour of the festival of St. George, was soon to be held at Saragossa, in the kingdom of Aragon. If the Don would ride thither, he said, he would without doubt win unheard-of renown in the lists, and gloriously overcome the knights of Aragon, which would be the same as overcoming the most famous knights of the world.

This the Don resolved to do, and there and then ordered Sancho Panza to go and prepare all things for his departure, which was to be in about eight days time. A few days went by, and the niece and housekeeper, who were all eyes and ears where the Don's affairs were concerned, soon imagined that another adventure was afoot. When Sancho appeared at the house again, and was locked up with his master, in private talk, for some time, the housekeeper could endure no longer, but, full of anxious suspicions, ran off to Carrasco's house and told him all her fears. He bade her not disturb herself, but return home, and he would follow her presently. She did so, and when she had left him the bachelor went to find the priest and to take counsel with him.

The result of this was, that when Carrasco arrived at Don Quixote's he did not, much to the housekeeper's anger and annoyance, try to turn the Don from his purpose. Instead, he urged him still further to ride forth again, and even offered to lend him a new helmet. The niece and housekeeper made the house ring with their laments, but all in vain. The knight now made up his mind to depart in three days, and therefore hastened his preparations; and the priest and Master Nicholas, being in a certain plot which they had devised with Carrasco, did not attempt to hinder him.

In three days all was ready. Don Quixote had succeeded in quietening his housekeeper and niece, and Sancho his wife (who had rated him for setting out a second time, declaring that the governorships of islands were not for such simple folk as they, and would bring them no good); and one evening, at dusk, the two set forth unobserved. They took the road to Toboso, for the knight had a mind to pay a visit to the lady of his heart before undertaking any other adventure in good earnest; and they were accompanied for a little way along the road by the bachelor Carrasco. He shortly bade them both farewell, however, begging the Don to send him an account of whatever fortune befell him, and then he returned to the village. The knight and his squire rode on towards Toboso, the one mounted on his faithful Rosinante and the other on his dear Dapple, the wallet of the squire being well stuffed with provisions, and his purse filled with money, with which his master had provided him, to supply all their wants.

That night and the next day passed without any adventure; and towards the second evening they saw the spires of Toboso appear in the distance across the plain. At the sight Sancho's heart went down to his shoes. For it will be remembered, that when he had been sent by his master to find Dulcinea before, he had never set eyes upon her, but had come back to the Don with a made-up tale about her sayings and doings. Therefore, he had no idea where she was now to be found, any more than had his master; and he knew not what he must do if he should be sent into Toboso in quest of her. Thus? though the knight was in high spirits at the thought of soon seeing his adored lady, the squire was utterly cast down because he had never seen her. Don Quixote made up his mind to enter the town at nightfall; and, until the darkness came, the two halted and rested in the shade of a grove of oak trees not far off.

When the night was come, they rode towards the town, and by the time they had reached it all was dark and silent as the grave, save for the barking of dogs, the braying of asses, and the grunting of pigs. They groped along the deserted streets for some little time; and at length Sancho, in answer to the knight's request to lead him to Dulcinea's palace, said:

"Since your honour will have it that it is a palace (though to me, at the time I visited it, it seemed no more than a little hut), let me take leave to ask you, is this an hour to find the gates open to us? And would it be seemly, think you, to stand hammering and thumping at the door in the middle of the night, and setting all the house a-bustle, as if we were belated travellers seeking admission at a common inn?"

"First of all," replied the Don, "let us find Dulcinea's palace, and then I will tell you what it will be proper to do and not to do. What is yonder bulk that looms up in the darkness? Methinks that must be no other than her palace itself."

"Lead on towards it, then, sir," replied Sancho, "perhaps it is, perhaps it is not; but I can tell you that if I were to see it and touch it, I would no more believe it to be what you say than I now believe that darkness has gone and day come."

They wandered on a few hundred paces farther, and presently came under the gloomy shadow of the building the Don had pointed out; when they discovered that it was no palace, but the chief church of the town, the great steeple soaring above them into the night sky.

"Sancho," said the knight, "we have got to the church."

"So I see, your worship," returned Sancho, "and let us pray Heaven that we have not got to our graves as well; it is a bad sign, to my thinking, to be wandering about churchyards at this time of night."

An hour or so more passed, and Dulcinea's palace remained still undiscovered, though the sky was by this time beginning to grow lighter with the coming dawn. Don Quixote was downcast at his ill-success, puzzled and uncertain; and the squire, seeing this, and wishing at all costs to get him out of the town before it was quite light, persuaded him at length to leave it, and take shelter again in some neighbouring grove. Then he himself, he said, would go back whilst his master rested, and leave not a stone unturned in all the place until he had found the lady and conveyed his master's duty to her, and besought her to see and to bless her faithful knight before he set forth upon his hazardous quest.

Don Quixote gladly agreed to Sancho's proposal; and by and by, about two miles from Toboso, they found a small wood, where the Don at once took shelter, bidding his squire return immediately to the town. He sent a thousand messages to his lady, urging Sancho to pay particular attention to her words and actions and looks when she received them.

"Trust me," said the wily fellow, "I will do all that is needful, and be back again quickly. And in the meantime keep up that sinking heart of yours, sir. 'A good heart sends bad luck packing,' you know; and likewise, 'Where we least think it, there starts the hare.' Which is as much as to say, that though we could not find madam's house in the darkness, yet I trust to find it ere I have looked for it, now that day has come."

Thus saying, he turned Dapple about and rode off, leaving his master thoughtful and sad in the midst of the grove. But the squire was in reality no less perplexed than the knight; for now he found himself in a most difficult position, and did not well know how he was to get out of it. Accordingly, he had no sooner lost sight of the Don between the trees, than he dismounted, cast himself down below a tree-trunk, and began to hold a solemn conversation with himself.

"Now, brother Sancho," said he, "where do you suppose you are going? To seek some ass that is lost? No, truly, but to find nothing less than a great lady, a princess. And where do you think to find her, then? In the great city of Toboso, to be sure. And who, pray, sent you a-princess hunting? Why, my master, the renowned Don Quixote de la Mancha, the knight who rights all wrongs, gives meat to the thirsty and drink to the hungry. Very well: where is this lady's house, Sancho? And have you ever seen her? My master says her house can be nothing less than some great palace or castle; and as for the lady, I have never set eyes on her in all my born days. Methinks, that to look for Dulcinea in Toboso is as bad as looking for a needle in a stack of hay. The mischief is in the whole matter! Well, now, this master of mine is clean out of his seven senses, as anybody with half an eye can tell; and, of a truth, I think I am almost as bad as he for following him and falling in with these whimsies of his, for: 'Show me thy company,' says the proverb, 'and I'll tell thee what thou art.' His wits are so far gone that he takes black for white and white for black (for ere now he has taken windmills for giants and flocks of sheep for armies); so I believe that I shall have no difficulty in persuading him that any country lass—the first one I shall clap eyes on, indeed—is my lady Dulcinea. And if he should swear that she is not, I will out-swear him that she is, and keep on declaring it, yea, and stick to it, whatever he says. And so he will be bound to believe it at last, and send me upon no more such fool's errands. Or else he will believe that some wicked enchanter, who bears him a grudge, as he says, has changed his lady's form into the form of a country lass, in order to spite him."

Having come to this conclusion, Sancho stayed where he was, and took his ease; nor did he make any attempt to return to the knight until evening, that the Don might think he had been in Toboso all the day.

Fortune favoured him when at last he decided to remount and go back, for he suddenly saw, coming towards him over the plain, three country damsels mounted upon three young asses. At the first view of them, up got the squire upon his Dapple, and galloped off to his master, with the news that the lady Dulcinea herself, with two of her fair maidens, was coming at that very moment to make his honour a visit. The love-lorn Don could hardly believe his ears; but Sancho urged him out of his retreat.

"Come on, sir, come on!" he cried, "and you shall see our princess her very self, all adorned, and her pretty damsels too, in cloth of gold, and pearls, and glittering diamonds, with their shining locks hanging over their shoulders like sunbeams in the sun. And, moreover, they are coming this way, every one mounted upon an ambling mule, the finest I have ever seen!"

"You mean an ambling palfrey, Sancho," corrected his master.

"It does not matter," quoth Sancho, "what they be; but they (the damsels, I mean) are sure the loveliest creatures that ever I set eyes on!"

All this time the squire was hurrying his master through the wood; and presently they came in sight of the country girls riding towards them along the road.

Don Quixote stared beyond them, and then asked his squire whether the ladies had got out of the city when he saw them?

"Out of the city!" cried Sancho. "Are your worship's eyes at the back of your head? Can you not see them riding towards us at this moment, for all the world like the sun on a May-day morning?"

"I can see nothing but three country girls mounted upon three asses," replied the perplexed knight.

"Oh, sir, do not say such a thing!" cried Sancho in a shocked tone, "but clear your eyes, and come and pay your duty to the beauteous lady of your heart."

By this time the two parties had met, and the squire rode forward to meet the damsels, casting himself down in the dust before the one who rode in the middle, and seizing her ass by the bridle.

"O magnificent princess and sun of beauty!" he cried. "Be pleased, of your graciousness, to look with favour upon your captive knight, who stands here all speechless, indeed, struck all of a heap, to find himself in the awesome presence of your beauteous and mighty princess-ship! I am nothing more than Sancho Panza, his squire, but he is the renowned Don Quixote de la Mancha, otherwise known as the Knight of the Sorrowful Figure!"

Don Quixote now knelt by his squire's side before the damsel, but he gazed upon her in a bewildered fashion, without saying a word. For, indeed, anything more unlike the graceful and dainty lady of his dreams could not well have been found in all Spain. The girl was a heavy, plump, and bouncing lass, with ruddy-purple cheeks, a flat nose, and a wide mouth. She and her companions, in their turn, stared in wonder at the two men kneeling before them; but at length she who had been addressed spoke in a hoarse voice.

"Get along with you both!" said she scornfully, "and be hanged to the pair of you for standing in our road! Let us pass, I say!"

"O fair princess and queen of Toboso," cried Sancho, "does not your high heart relent, to see the flower of knight-errantry down on his knees in the dust before you?"

Then one of the other damsels chimed in, and said to her companions: "How these small gentry folk, who think they are somebody in the world, take pleasure in making a mock of us poor country lasses, as if they thought we could not give back as good as we get! Get you gone on your own way, sirs, and we will go on ours; and so farewell, and plague take you for a couple of meddling mortals!"

Then, at last, Don Quixote spoke. "Rise up, Sancho," said he; "for I perceive that Fortune has not yet finished visiting her disasters upon me, and forbids me any comfort or relief. And thou, thou worthy and peerless fair, thou pearl among women, thou, whom some enchanter has changed into the form of a country lass to work me woe, dimming my eyes, and mine only, to thy beauty, hear my pleading now! If he has not by some evil chance done the same by me in thine eyes, and transformed me too, O look, then, I beseech thee, with one kind glance upon thine adoring knight, whose bended knees and piteous looks testify to the zeal with which he ever worships thee!"

"Stuff and nonsense!" quoth the country maid. "You keep your breath to cool your broth, my gentleman and let us go. and we will thank you for it!"

The wicked Sancho, highly delighted at the success of his plan, let go the girl's bridle; and no sooner did she find herself free than she whipped up her ass. The beast, resenting the blows, began to prance and kick with a will, and ended by bringing my lady Dulcinea headlong to the earth. Sancho and the Don ran to help her, but she was too quick for them. Getting on her feet, she gave a little run, grasped her ass by the crupper, vaulted into the saddle with one leap, and sat there astride. When her friends saw her thus, they cantered up to her, and in less than two moments the three were scouring away over the plain as fast as they could go, without once looking behind them.

The Don stared after them with all his eyes, until they were out of sight, then turned to his squire, sighing heavily.

"Now you see, my good fellow," he said, "how those evil enchanters of whom I have so often spoken have wrought me ill. For they have even deprived me of the sight of my own beauteous lady in her right and proper form—not granting me so much as that one favour. Alas! alas! I am the butt of all misfortune, and the most miserable of all men!"

Sancho replied with due solemnity; yet the whole while, as they presently took the road to Saragossa, the rogue was laughing in his sleeve, to think how easily he had been able to trick his too-confiding master.

2

The Knight of the Mirrors

Don Quixote rode upon his way, filled with melancholy to think of the sad enchantment of his Dulcinea, and racking his brains to find a device by which he might restore her to her proper form. Sancho consoled him as well as he could, by assuring him that, since the lady seemed to be enchanted to his eyes alone, the ill luck was probably more the Don's than Dulcinea's; and so long as she was blessed with health and contentment, they need not trouble themselves too much about the matter, but leave it to Time, the great healer of all ills, to mend this misfortune also.

Some hours later they encamped for the night in a pleasant grove of tall and shady trees. There they made a supper from the provisions in Sancho's wallet; and their two beasts were turned loose to graze as they would, or to lie down lovingly together as they often did, for Rosinante and Dapple were ever a couple of the most faithful friends.

Master and man presently fell asleep beneath the trees; but the Don had not been slumbering long when he was awakened by a sound quite near to him. He sat up, and, though he could see but little in the darkness, he made out the forms of two men dismounting from their horses, and heard one of them give orders to unbridle the beasts, at the same time casting himself upon the ground with a rattle of armour. By this Don Quixote made sure that some wandering knight-errant like himself had sought shelter in that place, and he waked Sancho at once, telling him that another adventure was at hand.

The two peered and listened in the dim light, and by and by discovered that the new-comers were a knight and his squire. The knight began to sing a melancholy love-song, and afterwards to call upon the name of her who was evidently his lady, bewailing her cruelty and declaring that he had caused her to be pronounced by all the knights of Spain the fairest beauty in the world. Don Quixote, hearing this, protested against it to his squire, and assured him that the strange knight was raving. The latter heard their voices, and, rising to his feet, spoke aloud in a courteous tone.

"Who goes there?" said he. "What are you? Are you of the number of the miserable, or the happy?"

"Of the miserable," answered our knight immediately.

"Come here to me, then," replied the other, "and tell me all your sorrows, and I will listen to them, and give you the tale of mine in return."

Don Quixote and Sancho went to him, and he made the Don sit beside him, and began to engage him in very civil talk. In the meanwhile the strange knight's squire took Sancho by the arm and led him aside that they, too, might talk together like their masters. They soon grew friendly over an immense pasty and a large bottle of wine supplied by the other squire—a meal which, it may be said, was very much to Sancho's liking, and to which he did full justice. After more friendly conversation they lay down where they were, and soon were fast asleep; but their masters had other matters to think of, for the strange knight was giving Don Quixote an account of his love for his chosen lady, whom he called the beauteous Casildea de Vandalia.

"She is a most hard-hearted fair one," said he, "for she sets me the most difficult and unheard-of tasks, that I may win her favour, and yet she ever withholds it from me. For her sake I have gone down into dreadful caverns in the abysses of the earth; for her I have lifted mighty stones that no other man could move; yea, for her sake I have even challenged and arrested the giantess Giralda, that weathercock of a woman, and made her stand still and look in my direction, and in my direction only, for a whole week at a time. And my lady's latest command is, that I should ride over the length and breadth of Spain, proclaiming her peerless beauty far and wide, and challenging and overcoming all who dare to call it in question. Thus I have already travelled far and vanquished many knights who presumed to set their own ladies' worth and beauty above that of my Casildea. Now I rejoice that my task is in a manner ended, and I am filled with pride and covered with glory, for in one of my combats I encountered and overthrew that far-renowned knight Don Quixote de la Mancha, who declared that the fairness of my Casildea was as nothing when compared with the beauty of his Dulcinea del Toboso. His fame is well known to be above the fame of all other knights; and so, having vanquished him, I look upon myself as the conqueror of all others; and the whole of his glory is transferred to me."

At this remarkable announcement Don Quixote, in his rage and amazement, was ready to fall upon the other furiously then and there, and make him take back his words; but he controlled himself.

"Sir," said he, "you may indeed have encountered and overthrown many of the knights of Spain, and when you tell me so I am ready to believe you. But that you have vanquished the knight Don Quixote de la Mancha I very much doubt. It may have been someone who bore his likeness (though there are not many such), but it certainly was not he."

"And why not?" demanded the other sharply. "I tell you I fought with him and overthrew him: I should know him anywhere; he is a lanky, longfaced, tall, grizzled gentleman, calling himself the Knight of the Sorrowful Figure, and he has for squire a fat country fellow called Sancho Panza. Moreover, the lady of his heart (whom he praised above mine) is named Dulcinea del Toboso. If you doubt my words further, sir, I am ready to make them good with this trusty sword of mine!"

"Calm yourself, sir," replied the Don, "and hear what I have to tell you. Don Quixote is the best friend I have in the world—were he myself I could not hold him dearer than I do—and by the description you give me, it certainly appears to be he himself whom you have forced to submit to you. But, on the other hand, I know by a thousand tokens of sight and feeling that it cannot possibly be the same, unless one of those evil-hearted enchanters, who plague him perpetually, has taken his shape and purposely been overthrown in his likeness, to cheat him of the glory which by rights belongs to that unlucky knight. And now, sir, if you do not believe my words behold Don Quixote de la Mancha himself before you, ready to prove the truth of his statement upon your body, with sword and lance, afoot or on horseback, or in whatever manner you think most fit!"

And as he spoke our valiant knight rose to his feet, and stood over the other menacingly, grasping his sword. Whereupon the strange knight answered:

"Señor Don Quixote, he who has once vanquished you in your enchanted shape may well hope to do so a second time when you wear your own proper form. But you know well that good knights-errant should not, like common robbers and rascals, fight out their differences in the darkness, as if they feared the fair light of day. Let us wait for the dawn, then, and when it comes I shall be ready to meet you hand to hand. And the condition of our combat shall be this: he who is worsted shall submit himself entirely to the commands of the conqueror, who shall do with him exactly as he chooses, provided that in whatever manner he shall dispose of him he shall in no way break or overstep the honourable laws of knight-errantry."

"I am contented, and will abide by this condition," replied Don Quixote. And thereupon the two went to wake their still snoring squires, and ordered them to prepare their horses for the coming combat.

Now the strange knight's squire declared to Sancho, that, as the masters were about to fall upon one another, it was only the proper thing for their men to do the same. But Sancho, who, as we know, was ever most tender of his own skin, did not see the force of this argument, and said so, with a good deal of wily reasoning and some bravado as well. Thus they waited for daylight; and, when it came, Sancho was filled with astonishment and not a little terror, to behold the strange squire's nose, which happened to be close to him. It was a huge and hideous feature, mulberry-coloured, covered with pimples, and hanging down far below his chin. Poor Sancho shook at the sight of it, and, resolving to endure anything ere he would awaken the wrath of such a frightful-looking creature, sidled away towards his master.

Meanwhile, Don Quixote, in the clear light was looking with much interest at his adversary. The latter was a well-made man, yet not very tall. His face was hidden by the beaver of his helmet, and he wore complete armour, over which was a surcoat of cloth-of-gold entirely besprinkled with tiny mirrors in the shape of half-moons, which glittered with his every movement, and made a most brilliant show in the newly-risen sun. A plume of green, white, and yellow feathers nodded abové his helmet; and his stout lance stood leaning against a tree. Don Quixote requested this gallant Knight of the Mirrors to lift up his beaver that his face might be seen, but the other courteously refused to do this until after the combat was over.

The two sprang upon their chargers, and wheeled them round for some distance to obtain each his vantage-ground. But before they had fully done so, the Knight of the Mirrors called to Don Quixote, who rode forward and met him half-way.

"Remember, sir," said the strange knight, the condition of the combat—that the conquered shall be wholly at the mercy and disposal of the conqueror."

"I remember it and will observe it," answered the Don, "provided that the conqueror's commands shall be no dishonour to the laws of chivalry."

Again they rode back to gain the full ground for their steeds' careers; but this time Sancho ran after his master, one hand grasping Rosinante's crupper.

"I beseech you, sir," he panted, "before you turn yourself about to set on, help me up into yonder cork-tree, that I may the better watch the fight."

"Oh, ho, Sancho!" replied his master, "I see you are anxious to get yourself out of harm's way."

"Nay, sir—'tis yonder squire's nose which sets my flesh a-creeping," was Sancho's whispered answer, "and I dare not for my life go anywhere near it!"

"It is, indeed, a most frightful object," said the Don, "and were I not the fearless knight I am, it would doubtless affright me too. Come, then, and I will help you into the tree."

Now while the Don was assisting his squire, the Knight of the Mirrors, having wheeled about, charged forward as fast as his steed would take him, which, indeed, was at a pace no swifter than poor Rosinante's own, being not much above a jog-trot. He had not noticed that Don Quixote was not advancing until he was well in the middle of his course, when he reined in his horse with a jerk. The beast, thankful to be pulled up, stood stock-still as if he never meant to move again. In the meanwhile the Don, having hoisted his squire into the tree, turned, clapped his spurs into Rosinante's flanks, and caused him to move forward with the nearest approach to a gallop that he had ever been known to make in all his life. But the unfortunate Knight of the Mirrors remained where he was, his steed refusing to budge an inch, and he himself fumbling awkwardly with his lance.

Don Quixote paid no attention to this, however, but charged on violently, with couched spear, and bore down upon his adversary with such speed and fury that in the force of his onset he thrust him heavily backward, and next moment had sent him sprawling from the saddle, head over heels, to the earth, where he lay motionless.

Sancho, as soon as he beheld his master victorious, slipped down from his perch, and ran to him. The Don dismounted, and strode over to the fallen knight to raise his helmet and give him air, if he still lived. Don Quixote lifted up the beaver, and as he did so gave a

loud cry of amazement. For the face of the Knight of
the Mirrors was no other than that of the bachelor
Samson Carrasco!

Immediately the Don called aloud to Sancho: "Come
hither, my son, and behold what those enchanters and
wizards can do!"

Sancho came and stood over the unconscious man,
stared all agape, then fell to crossing and blessing himself, and finally recommended the Don to put an end
to this particular work of wizardry at least, and perhaps to a wizard also, by thrusting his sword down his
victim's throat. His master was just about to take his
advice, when up rushed the strange squire with his
great nose gone.

"Ah, sir," he gasped earnestly, "have a care what
you do, for he who now lies senseless at your feet is
no more and no less than your neighbour, Samson
Carrasco, and I am his squire!"

"Why, where is your nose?" burst out Sancho, staring.

"Here, in my pocket," replied the other, and with
that he pulled out the horrible pasteboard mask which
had so disfigured him.

Sancho gazed and gazed the more; and at length,
unable to take his eyes off the fellow, cried out:

"Body o' me! If you are not mine own friend and
gossip, Tom Cecial, who dwells in our village! Are
you not, now, of a truth?"

"I am Tom Cecial, and no other," answered he of the
nose, "and presently I will tell you how I came to be

playing this fool's game here. But do beseech your master, Sancho, not to harm the Knight of the Mirrors who lies so helpless before him, for indeed and indeed, 'tis no other than Master Samson Carrasco, our countryman."

The unfortunate Knight of the Mirrors had by this time regained consciousness, only to feel Don Quixote's sword at his throat, and to hear him declaring he should die that instant if he did not at once confess that the glorious beauty of Dulcinea was far above that of every other maiden in the world, including his own Casildea. Moreover, said the Don, the fallen knight, being at his mercy, was bidden by him to go at once to Toboso, there to do homage before the lady Dulcinea. And besides all this, he must at once admit that the Don Quixote whom he had formerly vanquished was not Don Quixote at all, but someone in his likeness, "just as you," ended the Don, "though seeming in every feature to be the bachelor Samson Carrasco, are not he in reality, but someone who has been changed by the enchanters, my enemies, into Carrasco's form."

The other knight, sore and groaning, promised to confess and perform and admit all that was required of him; and got to his feet at last, to make his way out of the grove as best he could, along with his squire. Sancho, though he had asked a thousand questions of the squire, and been answered truly concerning who he was, could not yet assure himself that he was really his own gossip Tom Cecial; but was more than half inclined to think, with his master, that the whole puzzling business was the result of enchantment.

But the truth of the matter was indeed no other than this. The bachelor Samson Carrasco, with Thomas Cecial for his squire, had ridden out, with the full consent and approval of the good priest and Master Nicholas, in the guise of a knight-errant, to overtake Don Quixote upon his quest. The three friends had plainly seen that it was useless to hinder the Don from setting forth upon another mad ramble; yet at the same time, they thought and hoped that if Carrasco, disguised as a knight, could meet him, provoke him to combat, and overcome him, he might induce him to return home. For, they said, the condition of combat could easily be such as would render the vanquished one subject to whatever commands the victor should lay upon him. Don Quixote once overcome (and the three never dreamt of matters falling out otherwise), they knew he would strictly abide by the condition of combat, submit himself to his victorious opponent's will, and return quietly to his own village, as he would be commanded to do. There, they decided, he should be charged to stay for a space of two years or so, during which time they hoped that his frenzy would wear itself out, or else that something could be found to cure it once and for all.

However, as has been seen, their plans, by ill-fortune, went very much awry. The crestfallen Knight of the Mirrors, nursing his injuries and vowing vengeance some time or other upon Don Quixote for bringing him to such a pass, went off to find a bone-setter to mend his broken ribs.

Thomas Cecial accompanied him as far as the next village, and then left him, to return to his own home. As for the valorous Don Quixote de la Mancha and his faithful squire, they remounted their beasts, and rejoicing hugely at the Don's late successful exploit, continued their way towards Saragossa.

3

How Don Quixote outfaced a Lion

Some little time after Don Quixote's encounter with the Knight of the Mirrors, he and Sancho, in the course of their journey, met with a gentleman upon the high-road. He told them that his name was Don Diego de Miranda, and that he was riding home to his native village; and, after a little conversation with our knight, he begged him to accompany him and dine with him— an invitation which Don Quixote accepted.

As they were riding along together Don Quixote espied in the distance a kind of car coming towards them, drawn by mules and decorated with several small flags bearing the royal colours. Here, to the knight's romantic fancy, was another grand adventure!

He called aloud to Sancho to give him his helmet (for he had been riding without it), settled himself firmly in his saddle, grasped his lance more tightly, and declared himself ready to meet either man or demon.

Don Diego watched all this with an amused curiosity; and presently they were face to face with the car. Its driver was mounted upon one of the mules, and another man was seated upon the front of it. The knight rode forward, placed himself squarely before the newcomers, and demanded:

"Where are you going, my masters? Whose car is that, and what do you carry in it? And what are those banners that are waving above it?"

"The car is mine," answered the man upon the mule. "Inside it there are two fierce lions which the general of Oran is sending as a present to His Majesty the King, to whose court we are taking them even now. As for the flags, those are His Majesty's too, put here to show that what is in this car belongs to him."

"And are the lions large?" asked our hero.

"The largest, I dare swear, that ever came out of Africa into Spain," replied the man on the front of the car. "I am their keeper, and have had charge of many lions in my time, but never of any so immense as these. They are hungry just now, for as yet they have not been fed to-day; and therefore, sir, move yourself out of our way that we may be jogging on to the place where we are to feed them."

Don Quixote, however, merely sat still upon Rosinante and smiled.

"Lion cubs! Lion cubs!" he said. "To me! And at this time of day! By the word of a true knight, those who sent such creatures to encounter me shall soon know whether I am to be affrighted by the sight of a lion! Get you down, my friend, and as you are the beasts' keeper, open the cages and let them loose. For here in the open field I mean to show them who Don Quixote de la Mancha is, and how he will outface them, and those malicious enchanters whose hand he can plainly perceive in this adventure."

At this announcement Sancho ran round to Don Diego's side, beseeching him to induce the knight to give up such a hazardous undertaking as an encounter with freed and savage lions. "For if he carries out what he says we are all dead men," ended he.

"What!" said Don Diego. " Is your master so crazy that you really think he will attack these beasts?"

" He is not crazy," replied Sancho, "only somewhat rash, good sir."

Don Diego then went up to the knight, who was urging the reluctant keeper to open the cages, and tried to turn him from such a foolhardy purpose as he seemed bent upon, declaring that knights-errant might be as brave as they chose, but to behave in a manner so desperately rash was bordering upon madness. For all his pains, however, he got nothing more than a polite order to mind his own affairs and leave other men to mind theirs. Then Don Quixote turned again to the keeper.

"Sirrah," roared he, brandishing his lance threateningly before the fellow's nose, "if you do not instantly open that cage as I have commanded you, I vow by this hand that I will pin you to the car!"

The mule-driver, scared out of his wits at the words and the speaker's determined air, now begged leave to unharness his mules and take them safely out of harm's way ere the lions should appear. "For if my beasts are killed," whimpered he, "I am ruined, and my sole means of a livelihood gone for ever."

Don Quixote smiled in a pitying fashion. "O thou

man of little faith!" exclaimed he. "Unyoke thy beasts, if thou wilt, and get them away. But in a short time thou shalt see how vain all thy fear and labour have been!"

And now the keeper spoke. "Let all the company here bear witness," cried he, "that against my will and by force alone I let these lions loose. And moreover, I protest to this gentleman that he, and he only, shall be responsible for the damage they do, and for my wages also, if, as is well-nigh certain, I lose my post through this affair. Now, sirs, let all make haste to save themselves ere I open the cage doors. As for me, I fear no harm from the beasts, being their keeper."

In vain did Don Diego try to reason again and again with Don Quixote; in vain did Sancho pray his master with tears in his eyes to give up this adventure, which was like to prove the most disastrous he had yet undertaken. "Sure, your worship," wailed the squire, "there's no enchantment here, no, nor anything like it. I tell you I saw not a minute ago, through the bars of yonder cage, the paw of a real, live, flesh-and blood lion. And 'tis a paw of such hugeness that the beast it belongs to must be as big as a mountain, at least!"

"Fear renders it larger in your eyes, my friend," answered the knight loftily. "Now, Sancho, retire and leave me; and if I should perish in this enterprise, you know the ancient agreement between us: go to my Dulcinea—I will say nothing more."

Again he set himself firmly before the cages, and renewed his commands to the keeper to open the door.

Don Diego, the mule-driver and his mules, and Sancho, lamenting his master's folly aloud to the heavens, all made the best of their way to a place of safety, seeing that Don Quixote's resolution could in no way be shaken. When their backs were turned, the keeper dallied with the opening of the first cage, to argue once more with the valorous challenger of lions, who waved him away, and dismounted from Rosinante, drawing his sword and planting himself with much determination close to the cage. For he had no mind that Rosinante, at the sight of the animals, should take fright and run away with him; that staid beast not being, as he remembered, at all used to lions. And thus, alone and on foot, commending himself devoutly first to Heaven and then to his Dulcinea, our knight awaited the encounter.

Slowly the keeper, trembling for this crazy gentleman's safety, opened the cage door, disclosing to view an immense lion with a powerful lithe body, heaped-up yellow mane, and glowing, golden eyes. At the sound of the opening grate, the beast rose, turned himself round leisurely, put out one great paw, and stretched himself like a cat. Then he sat down at the cage entrance, yawned lazily several times, showing a crimson cavern of a mouth, and began to lick the dust from his face with nearly half a yard of tongue. When he had finished his toilette he blinked, thrust his head out of his cage, and gazed around him curiously with his yellow fires of eyes—a sight that might have aroused terror in the bravest heart. Don Quixote, however, stared at him steadily all the while, only wishing that the beast would leap from his cage so that he might grapple with him and fight him to the death.

But the lion had no such intention. Calmly he took stock of all there was to be seen without, and then, paying not the slightest attention to the war-like figure standing defiantly under his nose, he coolly turned his back upon the outside world and everything in it, and flopped down again on his side in the cage.

Then Don Quixote, watching him, ordered the keeper to rouse him with blows, if nothing else would serve, to make him come forth.

"Nay, now," replied the fellow stoutly, "that is what I will not do. For if I rouse him to wrath, I shall be the first one he will tear in pieces. Be satisfied, sir, that all has been done that could be required of the bravest. There was his majesty, there were you, there was the open door through which he could have come had he chosen; yet he did not choose, nor, I dare engage, will he come out all this day. Now, as I understand the matter, no combatant is expected to do more than challenge his foe and await his appearance in the field; and if that foe comes not, then the shame is his, and the glory all the challenger's."

"Why, that is true enough," replied the Don. "Fasten the door of the cage, my friend; and then bear witness to the others, as soon as they return, concerning all that has taken place."

He then signalled to his squire, to Don Diego, and to the muleteer, who all this time had been making off over the plain with their heads over their shoulders and their eyes on the car, in their curiosity to know what was taking place there.

At the sight of the Don's white handkerchief fluttering on his lance they turned and retraced their steps, slowly at first, but presently more rapidly, full of wonder to see the knight still alive and unharmed. When they came up, the keeper gave them a full and highly-coloured account of the knight's exploit and the lion's behaviour, and told them how Don Quixote, wanting nothing in valour, would have had the beast provoked a second time to come forth, but that he, the keeper, would not do it.

Then Don Quixote said: "What think you of all this, son Sancho? Truly, those enchanters may try their arts upon me, but, in the face of my unshaken courage and resolution, though they may take good fortune from me many a time, yet they cannot overcome me, as you see. Give these good fellows a gold piece each, Sancho, to compensate them for the time I have caused them to lose. And you, friend muleteer, fasten your beasts to the car in security, and go on your way again."

The keeper of the lions thanked the knight humbly for his generous gift, and promised to relate the whole wonderful incident to the King himself when he reached the court.

"And if you do so, my friend," replied Don Quixote, much gratified, "and if His Majesty inquires who performed this deed, tell him that 'twas Don Quixote de la Mancha, the Knight of the Lions; for this is the honourable title I now take upon myself, in place of that of the Knight of the Sorrowful Figure. And in so doing I follow the ancient practice of knights-errant of old, who changed their names whenever it pleased them, or whenever it was to their advantage so to do."

4

The Enchanted Bark

Many other remarkable adventures, both pleasant and unpleasant, befell Don Quixote and his squire after the knight's encounter with the lion. Some days later he descended alone into the far-famed Cave of Montesinos, which was situated in the heart of the country of La Mancha, and there he saw, or said he saw, a host of marvellous things amongst them his lady Dulcinea, enchanted still, he declared, as she had been when he met her outside Toboso in the form of a country lass.

Then, his high-flown notions of chivalry carried him away, and rendered him even more ridiculous than usual, one evening at an inn. There came to the place a stroller with a puppet-show, which he set up for the entertainment of the inn-guests. The puppets were made to act the story of the knight Gayferos freeing his wife Melisendra from the hands of the Moors. This performance so excited the valiant Don that he took the puppets to be no less than flesh and blood; and when the Moors set upon Gayferos and his lovely lady our knight rose up, and began to lay upon the pagans, cut and thrust and slash, with his sword, until the pasteboard figures were most of them beheaded, and the whole puppetshow destroyed by his onslaught.

The knight paid handsomely for the ruin he had

wrought, and, with Sancho, took the road again; for he meant to visit the banks of the river Ebro before he entered Saragossa.

A few days afterwards they came in sight of the famous river, a clear, smooth, broad stream, running pleasantly and gently between wooded meadows. Don Quixote gazed about him with delight, but his joy grew greater when he beheld upon the waters a little boat, with neither oars nor tackle, moored to a tree that grew upon the river-bank. Not a soul was in sight save the knight and his squire; and, having looked all round him carefully, Don Quixote dismounted and commanded Sancho to do the same, bidding him tie both their beasts fast to the willow-tree upon the water's brink. Sancho asked the reason for this order, and the knight stood before him and answered:

"Know, Sancho my son, that this bark is waiting for me, in order that I may enter it at once and set out upon some worthy adventure of which at present I have no knowledge, but which is probably to bring aid and comfort to some captive knight or high-born person who is in distress. For that is the way of all enchanters in books of chivalry, when some knight or other finds himself in serious difficulty from which he cannot be freed save by the efforts of another knight. Though the rescuer should be many thousand leagues away from the one to be rescued, yet the enchanters will waft him, either through the clouds or over the water, in the twinkling of an eye, to that place where his help is required. So, you see, this bark is floating here for no other purpose than to carry us away upon a new quest. Fasten up our beasts, therefore, and follow me, and may Heaven guide us; for I will go aboard though a host of holy men should entreat me on their knees to stay."

"Well, since you will have it so," said Sancho, shrugging his shoulders but preparing to do as he was told, "there is no course, I suppose, but to obey your worship, if you will for ever be running after these odd whimsies of yours. 'Do as thy master bids thee', says the proverb, 'even should he bid thee sit down by him at the board.' But all the same, I am sure this boat belongs not to any enchanters, but to fishermen; for in these waters are caught the best shads that ever were found." And with a very long face indeed he tied Rosinante and his ass to the tree, leaving them to the mercies of whatever enchanter might choose to look after them.

His master, seeing his doleful countenance, bade him comfort himself; for, he said, the enchanter who was to carry the men through regions of such longitude would not fail to care for the poor beasts left behind.

"I have no notion what your longitudes mean," grumbled Sancho. "I am sure I never heard such a word in all my born days."

"Longitude means length," answered the Don, smiling, "and no wonder that you do not know the word, for you are not bound to understand Latin. Though some there are, indeed, who pretend to a knowledge of it, yet know no more than you, my friend."

"Well, sir, what are we to do next?" asked Sancho.

"Do?" was his master's reply. "Why, embark, and cut the rope." Which, without further delay he did, Sancho following him closely.

Set adrift, the boat and its occupants glided gently out into the open stream; but it had gone no more than a couple of yards from the bank before Sancho began to tremble in fear. It was hard to say which oppressed him most, the terror of being upon the water in an oarless boat, or the fact that he was every moment drifting farther away from the ass and horse on the land, one of which faithful beasts was braying pitifully, and the other tugging at his fastenings to get loose.

"Alas, alas!" wailed Sancho. "Hear how my Dapple brays after me, and see how poor Rosinante is struggling to get free and follow us! Oh, oh, dearest friends, stay in peace and safety; and may this madness which parts us from you turn quickly to reason and a sense of our own foolishness, and bring us speedily back to you!"

His words were accompanied by an outburst of noisy weeping which irritated his master exceedingly, and drew down a rebuke upon the squire's head.

"What are you afraid of, chicken-heart?" said the knight scornfully. "What are you weeping for? Who is hurting you? Who pursues you, soul of a mouse? Do you lack for anything now? Are you undergoing great hardships, trudging barefoot over rugged mountain-passes? No, indeed, but seated easily upon a bench like a prince upon his throne, gliding gently down this delightful river which presently will carry us out to the unfathomable ocean. Nay, without doubt we have got out even now, and must have travelled at least seven or eight hundred leagues. By this time I am certain that we have passed, or are just about to pass, that equinoctial line which divides the poles."

"And when we have got to that line your honour speaks of," sniffed Sancho, sitting up, "how far shall we have gone then?"

"Why, a great distance," was the Don's answer. "For the whole globe contains three hundred and sixty degrees, according to the computation of the famous geographer Ptolemy; and when we have travelled one half of it we shall come to the equinoctial line."

"Faith!" replied Sancho, round-eyed. "He must have been a clever fellow, that same Tolmy What's-his-name, with his amputation, to vouch for the truth of all that you tell me, sir."

His master smiled at Sancho's blundering simplicity; and the little boat floated slowly and steadily on. After a short time the two adventurers saw one or two tall water-mills in the midst of the river; and no sooner had the Don set eyes on them than he called aloud to his companion:

"Behold, my friend! There before you stands the fortress wherein is imprisoned the distressed knight or lovely princess to whose succour I have been sent!"

"What fortress does your worship talk of?" asked Sancho, staring. "Can you not see that yonder is only a group of water-mills for the grinding of corn?"

"Peace, Sancho," was the knight's reply. "Though they seem to you to be mills, they are in reality no such thing. How many times have I assured you that enchanters, by their arts, and whenever they will, can change the appearance of everything, so that nothing is what it seems? Remember the transformation of my dear Dulcinea, sole star of my life!"

The boat had now drifted into the current of the river, and was heading, at a more rapid speed than hitherto, towards the mill-stream. The millers had been watching it; and now, seeing that it was being swiftly borne by the current to the great mill-wheels, they rushed out, all floury as they were, to stop its progress with poles.

"Hi, hi!" they bellowed to the two in the boat. "What the mischief are you doing, and where are you going? Do you want to drown yourselves, or be ground in pieces by the wheels?"

But the knight, bidding Sancho look on, and giving not the least thought to the disaster he was fast heading for, stood up majestically in the wildly-rocking boat, and called aloud to the whitened millers:

"Goblins or demons, rascals and scoundrels, whatever ye be! I demand that you shall at once set at liberty that person, whether of high or low estate, whom you keep a captive in yonder fortress. For know that I am Don Quixote de la Mancha, otherwise known as the Knight of the Lions, for whom, by order of high Heaven, is reserved the glorious ending of this adventure!"

And with that he drew his sword and began to make violent passes in the air, as if he had been fighting all the millers in a body. But they, understanding neither his gestures nor his talk, rushed to stop, with their poles, the helpless craft which was even then being drawn into the eddy of the swift stream.

Sancho, his hair standing on end with fright, fell on his knees in the bottom of the boat, and prayed for a speedy deliverance from peril—a prayer which was soon answered, for the millers, setting their stout poles against the boat, stopped it in mid-stream. The arrest was so sharp and sudden, however, that the bark swerved, dipped, and finally turned clean over, throwing the knight and his squire into the river.

Happily, Don Quixote was as much at home in the water as a duck; yet the weight of his armour bore him down to the bottom of the river twice; and had not the millers thrown themselves into the water and buoyed up the two adventurers, they would certainly have been drowned.

When they were hauled on to dry land, more wet than thirsty, Sancho's first act was to fall upon his knees and beseech Heaven to save him from any share in his master's future mad escapades. The enchanted bark, left to its fate, had drifted beneath the mill-wheels and was splintered to matchwood; and now up came some fishermen, who turned out to be its owners. At the sight of it, they fell in a fury upon poor Sancho, and demanded instant payment for the loss of their craft.

Very calmly, as if nothing out of the ordinary had occurred, Don Quixote told both the fishermen and the millers that he would most willingly pay for the boat, upon condition that the captive persons in the castle should be freely delivered up to him.

"What are you saying, madman?" cried the millers. "And what captives and castle are you talking about? Would you be running away with the good folk who come to grind their corn at our mills?"

"It is enough," thought the Don, shrugging his shoulders at this latest stupidity of the rabble. "Who can expect this wooden-headed mob to do aught that is honourable? Surely there are two enchanters at work in this matter: one carries me hither in his fairy bark; the other outwits him by oversetting it, and me, and his plans for me, all together and at once. The world is full of tricks and plots and counter-plots. Heaven help us! I can do no more than I have done!"

With these thoughts, he turned his face to the mills, and called aloud:

"My friends, whoever you may be, who are held captive in prison there, pardon me that, through no fault of mine own, I am unable to deliver you from your distresses this day. This adventure is reserved for some other knight than poor Don Quixote!"

He then turned to the fishermen and settled the affair of the destroyed boat, ordering Sancho to pay out fifty reals to its owners by way of compensation. This the squire did very unwillingly, grumbling and remarking that two more such embarkations would sink the whole of his master's small capital.

The millers and the fishermen gaped and stared at the master and man, not understanding the knight's speeches in the least, but taking the two for nothing more than a couple of crazy fellows; and presently they left them, and went back to their mills and huts.

Don Quixote and Sancho, much bedraggled and downcast, returned to Rosinante and Dapple, mounted their beasts silently, and rode away, leaving the river Ebro behind them. And so ended the adventure of the enchanted bark.

5

How the Knight and his Squire were nobly entertained

And now a host of most marvellous and unexpected incidents occurred in the adventures of our hero and his honest squire. For the very day after the affair of the enchanted bark, the knight and his follower met a noble lady, a duchess, and her husband, who was one of the wealthiest dukes in the country. The two had heard all about Don Quixote and his surprising deeds, and they received him with much courtesy. They were, however, a merry couple, who loved innocent jests above all things; they were quick to observe the knight's craziness and the squire's simplicity, and had a mind to amuse themselves at the expense of both, while receiving both master and man in their stately mansion and treating them with the most kindly hospitality.

The duke, therefore, gave orders to all his servants, and especially to his head steward, that Don Quixote, during his visit, was to be treated exactly as a knight-errant of former days, with all the honour and ceremony which were due to a knight's rank. The duchess immediately took a fancy to Sancho Panza and his quaint, outspoken way of expressing himself in and out of season; and, all the time of his visit, she delighted in talking to him and having him near her. Don

Quixote was much gratified at his reception in the
duke's halls, not being at all used to having such great
courtesy shown to him. Indeed, he was now quite certain, for the first time in his career, that he was an
actual knight-errant; being, as he had never been before, treated in every way like a gallant and high-born
knight of old. As for Sancho, he wormed himself into
the noble company upon every occasion, in spite of all
his master's frowns and reproofs, attached himself to
the merry duchess, and, all unwittingly, afforded both
her and her husband endless amusement.

The duke, hearing all about Sancho's ambition to
have an island to govern as soon as Don Quixote should
win one to give him, promised him, in the name of his
valorous master, that he would give him one of his
own, which was at that time vacant. Sancho's delight,
of course, knew no bounds at this; and when he was
very gravely charged by the duchess to take heed how
he governed his subjects, he winked and said:

"Go to, your ladyship; I am an old dog, and understand. 'None will dare the loaf to steal from him that
shifts and kneads the meal.' The good shall have both
heart and hand of mine, but the bad neither foot nor
footing. Heaven's help is better than an early rising;
which is as much as to say, that with the aid of Providence and the best will in the world I shall no doubt
govern my island better than a goshawk. Ay, now—let
them put their fingers into my mouth, and they shall
see whether I know how to bite or no!"

The duchess was told by Sancho, as a great secret,

the whole truth about the marvellous enchantment of
the fair Dulcinea. Whereupon she and her husband,
with the help of their vassals and their steward, made
up an elaborate jest that should deceive the unsuspecting knight still further in this matter, and should, at the
same time, much disturb the squire's peace of mind.

One evening, therefore, when the ducal party and
their two guests had been the whole day hunting in the
woods, and had finished their sport, they were greatly
amazed, the duke and duchess in pretence and the
knight and squire in reality, to behold a most curious
scene. The forest was suddenly alive with the light of
many torches and the shrill sound of clarions, trumpets,
and fifes. Several cars, bearing hideous and fantastic
figures, passed before the group of watchers, to Sancho's
terror and the Don's never-ending wonder. Then came
a car, larger than the others, draped all in white, ablaze
with torches, and carrying a tall veiled figure which
called itself the arch-enchanter Merlin; and also a very
beautiful and bespangled lady (one of the duke's pages)
who posed as the fair and unhappy Dulcinea.

Merlin stood up in the car when it came opposite the
duke's open-mouthed guests, threw off his veil, and
disclosed the face and figure of a horrible skeleton. He
then declared, in a poetic speech, that Dulcinea's woeful plaints upon her transformation into an ugly country lass had summoned him from the shades. And he
now appeared, he said, to announce what must be done
in order to restore her to her original form. This change
could only be performed by Sancho Panza, the squire

of the renowned knight Don Quixote de la Mancha, who must give himself three thousand three hundred lashes with the whip so that the damsel might be freed from the cruel enchantment under which she lay.

And now Master Sancho, in spite of his terror, found voice enough to raise in indignant protest.

"Three thousand lashes!" cried he. "I would as soon stab myself to death three times! Lash myself, forsooth! Not I, if I know it! What has my poor tender skin got to do with any enchantments, pray? Nay, if Madam Dulcinea can find no other way to get herself disenchanted, she may go on being enchanted to her last hour, for me!"

Then his master, in great grief and rage, declared that if no other way would serve to make him do as he was bidden, he himself would tie him to a tree and give him the lashes with his own hand. But Merlin gravely said that that might not be so, for Sancho must receive every one of the lashes of his own free will, unforced; and moreover, he might take his own time about his whipping, and make up the tale of lashes in as few or as many days as it pleased him.

Then the supposed Dulcinea added her commands to those of Merlin; and finally the duchess said: "What do you say to all this, Sancho?"

"Say, madam?" cried the wrathful squire, "why, just what I have said before, and not a jot less; and as for the lashes, I pronounce them all!"

"'Renounce', you mean, Sancho," said the duke, "and not pronounce."

"Let me alone, your grandeur," was the poor squire's reply. "How is a body to think about the niceness of words, or of a letter more or less when one is so plagued that one knows not what one does, with the thought of lashes for ever in a body's mind?"

"Sancho," said the duke solemnly, lifting a finger at him, "if you do not give way, and consent to your honoured master's desire, I declare there shall be no island for you. Remember, therefore—no lashes, no government."

The squire's face lengthened at that; and he pleaded hard for a couple of days in which to consider the matter. But this the mock Merlin would by no means allow: Sancho's decision must be given then and there. So finally, when his friend the duchess had added her reasonings and entreaties to those of the rest of the company, Sancho gave way, and consented to lash himself for the sake of the fair Dulcinea and his master. But, he said, he must be permitted to lay on whenever he pleased, without being tied to days or times. And moreover, he bargained 'that he should not be bound to draw blood with the whip, and if some of the lashes chanced to be no more than fly-flaps, why, they should be counted just the same.'

Don Quixote fell upon his squire, kissed and embraced him, and gave him a hundred thanks for his noble act of generosity. All the company, hugely entertained, clustered about him in joy; the wonderful car with its occupants moved on and vanished; and the whole party presently returned home.

Many other amusing and innocent tricks were played by the duke and duchess upon their unsuspecting guests before Sancho went to take up his promised government. Yet the whole time the knight and squire, especially Don Quixote, were treated with the utmost courtesy. For his host and hostess saw that our hero, in spite of his crazy notions, was a well-bred gentleman, with a great deal of sense and true wisdom when chivalry and knight-errantry were not in question.

One of the things which afforded the mirth-loving couple much merriment was the manner in which Don Quixote was wrought upon by a clever piece of play-acting and an elaborate tale, made up by their steward, who was as waggish as they were. The steward, acting the part of a much-afflicted lady, came to Don Quixote with a pitiful tale of how she had been enchanted by a magician and giant whom she called Malambruno. This enchantment could only be removed, she declared, by Don Quixote, to whom she gave the title of "the valorous Manchegan, the world-renowned flower of knight-errantry." He, she said, must be her deliverer, and meet the enchanter Malambruno in single combat; and in order to do this he must mount, with his squire Sancho Panza behind him, upon the famous wooden horse named Clavileño. Clavileño was so called because he bore in his forehead a wooden peg by which his rider guided him instead of by a bridle; he could fly through the air swifter than the wind, and he would bear the knight and squire to the far-distant place where Malambruno was.

This fantastic story Don Quixote believed without question. A great horse of wood was brought into the duke's castle gardens; then the Don and Sancho were blindfolded and mounted upon it, the Don most calmly and courageously, and Sancho with much inward quaking and a good deal of unwillingness. For both were convinced that they were to be borne at once through leagues of space, to meet they knew not what perils.

Don Quixote turned the wooden peg in his steed's head, and immediately imagined, and assured Sancho, that they were being wafted away in mid-air. A crowd of delighted watchers had gathered in the gardens, where, silent as ghosts, but scarcely able to contain their laughter, they heard the master and man arguing about the distance they had already travelled, and telling each other that they had now certainly passed the second region of air, and had reached the region of fire above it. (The duke's mischievous servants had blown upon them silently with several immense pairs of bellows; and then warmed them up by thrusting before them great pieces of lighted flax fixed to the end of long canes.)

Sancho's curiosity was just about to get the better of his fear, and he had loudly announced his intention of peeping to see how far Clavileño had really travelled, when, with the suddenness of a gunshot and with a tremendous report, our two adventurers were sent flying up into the air in reality. They presently landed on the castle lawn, more scared and singed than hurt. For a piece of flaring flax, purposely put to Clavileño's tail, had set fire to a collection of squibs and firecrackers inside him, and caused this terrifying explosion.

The travellers were at first much bewildered to find themselves in the same garden from which they had set out. But when a mysterious scroll was discovered, announcing that the adventure of the afflicted lady and the wooden horse was now achieved, and that the enchanter Malambruno was satisfied, Don Quixote, though mystified, was content. As for the duke and duchess, they praised him to the skies as the most courageous and gallant knight-errant who ever lived; and amused themselves for some time thenceforward by listening to Sancho's account of his most marvellous, romantic, and unheard-of adventures in the regions of air and fire.

6

*Sancho's Government,
and how he left it*

And now the merry duke, being determined to carry
his Jest as far as he possibly could, bade Sancho make
ready to set forth to take up his government speedily;
for, he said, his future subjects were longing for his
presence. At the same time he gave all instructions to
his steward and many of his other followers concerning their behaviour to Sancho in his mock governorship, together with strict orders that they were to relate
to him everything that the new governor said and did.

Accordingly, a few days later, Sancho left the duke's
castle with his attendants, after receiving the farewells
and good wishes of his host and hostess, and a most
tender and affectionate blessing from his master, Don
Quixote—a moving parting which caused poor honest
Sancho to weep bitterly. He had already received from
the Don a number of very wise and well-expressed
maxims regarding the manner in which he, as a just
and worthy governor, should rule his island—maxims
which did honour to the knight's sense and intelli-
gence, and which Sancho faithfully promised to observe.

Behold our Sancho, then, very finely attired, well
attended, and mounted upon a beautiful mule, setting

forth upon the greatest adventure of his life. He was followed by his beloved Dapple, who, no less fine than his master, was led immediately behind him, furnished with handsome silken trappings. The sight of his darling pleased Sancho so much that he could scarcely take his eyes from him, but rode most of the way with his head over his shoulder, filled with admiration; and in that hour the new governor would not have exchanged places with the Emperor himself.

The so-called island proved to be a good town of about a thousand inhabitants, one of the best of its kind in the duke's possession. Sancho was given to understand that this was the island of Barataria; and therefore he was content to ask no questions concerning the nature of his kingdom—island or mainland, 'twas all one to him.

Upon his arrival, the town magistrates, the other dignitaries, and a great crowd of citizens, came forth to bid their new governor welcome. Amid many rejoicing shouts and much bell-ringing, they led him at once to the church to return thanks, afterwards presented him with the keys of the town, and solemnly established him as perpetual governor.

Then he was conducted to the court of justice, where he was requested to decide some rather puzzling matters. But before he did so, Sancho's eye caught some large letters written on the wall opposite his great chair of state. Being unable to read, he asked what they were, and was told that they said: "Upon this day (day, month, and year being named) Señor Don Sancho Panza took possession of this island, and long may he enjoy it."

"Look you," was Sancho's sturdy reply, "my name is plain Sancho Panza, as was my father's and grandfather's before me, without any garnishing of Dons or Donas. Doubtless there are more Dons than stones in this island, and if that be so, and my government lasts, I must be weeding them out forthwith. Now, Señor Steward, let us get to business."

Presently two men, a tailor and a countryman, entered the justice-court. Both saluted the governor, and then the tailor said that some days before, the countryman had come to him with a piece of cloth, asking him if it would make a cap. He had replied that it would, and was thereupon asked if it would make two, then three, then four, and, finally, five caps. He answered that five caps could certainly be made from the cloth; and five caps had accordingly been fashioned; yet, now that they were completed, the countryman, he complained, not only refused to pay for them, but demanded that either the cloth or the price of it should be returned to him.

"Is this the truth, brother?" asked Governor Sancho, turning to the country fellow.

"It is, my lord. But ask him to show the caps he has made for me," answered the man.

Then, amid the laughter of the court, the tailor pulled from his pocket five tiny caps which exactly fitted his four fingers and thumb, and, twirling them about, said:

"Here are the caps, my lord, properly fashioned; and

I swear before all the world that not a shred of the cloth is left."

The new governor thought for a moment, then gave his decision.

"'Tis no difficult matter, methinks, to settle this," said he. "I pronounce, that the tailor shall lose the cost of his work (since such work it is) and his customer the cost of his cloth. As for the caps, they shall be set apart for the use of the poor of the parish; and so there's an end of the whole affair, my masters."

The company's admiration for the new governor's wisdom had not abated ere two more men came before him with another grievance. They were both elderly, and one of them carried a tall cane as a staff. The one who had no staff told his tale, which was, that some time before, he had lent the other ten gold crowns, upon condition that they should be returned when demanded. When, at last, he asked for the return of the loan, his debtor told him that he had already paid him; yet there was neither fact nor witness to prove such a thing. He now requested that the debtor should be put upon his oath, and if he swore in Heaven's sight that the money had been returned, his creditor was willing to discharge him.

"Well, what do you say to all this, old gentleman of the staff?" inquired the governor.

"Hold down your rod of justice, my lord," was the old man's reply, "and I will swear upon it that I have paid my debt to this man."

Down went Sancho's rod, and at once the old man

gave his staff to his creditor to hold whilst he swore his solemn oath that he had paid him the money with his own hand. The creditor, much puzzled, but without more ado, accepted the oath; the old gentleman took his staff again, bowed to the governor, and left the court.

Then Sancho, head in hand, sat thinking deeply for some moments, after which he commanded that the old gentleman should be brought back into his presence.

"Give me that staff, my friend," said he, as soon as the other appeared; and then, when the staff was delivered to him, he handed it to the creditor.

"Go your ways, my master," he said. "For you are paid indeed."

"What, my lord!" cried the man. "Is this cane worth ten gold crowns, then?"

"Ay, marry, is it," was the governor's answer, "or I have no head to direct a government." And, taking the cane again, he broke it in two, and out rolled the gold pieces, one by one, to the wonder of all the company, who took their sage new governor for nothing less than a second Solomon.

Many wise and witty decisions did Sancho make in the justice-court until the business of the day was finished, and dinner-time came. The governor sat down to table in lonely state, with a pleased eye on the different kinds of delicious food that covered the board. But a long-faced individual, whom he was afterwards told was the governor's physician, stood sentinel over him with a rod in his hand, pounced upon each dish that caught poor Sancho's fancy, and ordered it to be borne away. For the good of his lordship's health, quoth master doctor, he must eat but little, and that little must be plain. So the fruit was removed because it was too acid and moist, the meat because it was too hot and too highly seasoned, the partridges because partridges could not possibly be good for anyone's stomach; and Sancho, hungry and longing, was advised to dine safely off a few wafers and a little marmalade.

This last counsel was too much for our governor, who, as we know, loved to dine well whenever he could. Indignant and enraged, he ordered the physician out of the hall, declared that he would clear the island of him and all his kind, and swore that an office that could not find a man in sufficient food and drink was not worth two beans.

He fared rather better at supper, and afterwards went the rounds, deciding more difficult questions with much native shrewdness and wit. And so the days of his governorship went by; and he began to find, before he had been in it a week, that such an office was by no means all that he had imagined. He made some sensible rules, however, for the good government of his so-called island—rules so praiseworthy that the chronicle says they are observed in the kingdom of Barataria to this day. Yet, he declared that he had never a moment to himself, that he was at the beck and call of his islanders all day long, even at meal-times; and as to feeding, why, he was half-starved by that rascal of a physician.

At length, one night, when he had gone to bed thoroughly tired, and hungry as usual, he was awakened by a terrible sound of bells ringing, trumpets braying, drums beating, and anxious voices calling him. He rose, went to his chamber door, and there beheld a company of his followers rushing towards him down the corridor, with torches and drawn swords.

"Arm, Señor Governor! Arm! arm!" cried they. "Arm, and lead us forth to victory, for the enemy is at our gates! Be our captain and our champion, for if you do not rise to our aid we are ruined and all dead men!"

The late squire was understood to say, above the clamour, that such matters were better left to his master, Don Quixote; and that he knew not how to deal with such alarms and bustles. But his words went unheeded; and at last his followers armed the quaking governor in two huge steel targets which they had brought for the purpose. These they bound tightly upon him, one before and the other behind him, till only his head and arms and toes were visible, and he looked like a tortoise in its shell. He was then handed a lance, and requested to march forth to victory.

"March!" wailed the unhappy man. "How in the world do you suppose I can do that, when I am held like a rasher of bacon between two plates? Alack, alack! I can hardly breathe, let alone march!" Yet the reproaches of his followers at last forced him to move a step, whereupon he stumbled and fell, coming down with a crash to the floor.

There he stayed, whilst the noise and shouting increased, the torches were extinguished, and, to add to his pain and fear, men began to trample upon him as he lay in his armoured shell with head and feet huddled close up to escape hurt if he could.

"Guard the postern! Down with the scaling-ladders! To the fore with your pitch and boiling oil, lads! This way, this way!" bellowed the voices about him in the darkness, as he was kicked and stumbled over and jumped upon in the mock mêlée.

"Oh," thought Sancho, "if I were but once clear of this unlucky island, and had left it for ever behind me!"

But at last he heard a cry of "Victory! The enemy flies! Rise, Señor Governor, and enjoy the conquest you have won!" Whereupon, with a faint and doleful voice, he bade them help him to get to his feet; and then, when he was unarmed and seated in a dazed fashion once more upon his bed, he swooned away with pain and terror.

This turn of affairs somewhat alarmed his roguish followers, who had really intended no harm by the trick they had played upon him. Presently, however, Sancho came to himself, and asked what hour it was. They told him it was daybreak; and to this he made no reply, but slowly rose from his bed, and, in a dead silence, began to dress himself, the steward and the other servants watching him in wonder.

When he had put on his clothes as well as he was able (for he was bruised all over, and shaking from head to foot), he limped down to the stable, the others following him in bewildered silence. They saw him make his way to the faithful Dapple's stall, saw him take the good creature's head in his arms and kiss him upon the forehead, and then begin to harness him tenderly.

"Come to me, dear friend and partner in all my woes and hardships," they heard him say. "When thou and I were companions day after day, when I had no other cares but the care to house thee and to feed thee—ah, then was I happy indeed! But since I left thee, to indulge my foolish pride and ambition, I have known nothing but pains, anxieties, and miseries for my folly."

By this time the little ass's harnessing was completed, and his master got stiffly upon his back, and then spoke gravely to the steward, the physician, and all the others who stood around watching him.

"Make way for me, gentlemen," said he. "And let me go whence I came, from bondage to liberty once more, from death to life again. Now I know that I was not born to be a governor: I understand digging and pruning, ploughing and reaping, in garden and field, better than the making of laws for an island, or the fighting of its enemies. Let St. Peter bide at Rome; every man to his own way of life, that is to say, and let him not be breaking his neck to take the way of another. I had rather eat my humble bowlful of porridge than sit before a rich table watched over by a meddling doctor who would fain starve me to death. I had rather lie cool beneath an oak-tree's shade in summer, and snug under a double sheepskin in winter, than remain, under the toils of a government, in silken sheets, and go clothed in sables. Heaven be with you all, good sirs. Say to my lord the duke that empty-handed I came, empty-handed I go; I neither win nor lose; I entered this government penniless, I go away the same, as an honest governor should do. And now let me be gone, that I may mend my bruises and the broken ribs which I have got, thanks to the enemies who were stamping upon me all the night through."

All entreated him to stay, but Sancho was firm. Their requests came too late, he said; such tricks could not be played twice; moreover, he was of the race of the Panzas, who were all headstrong, and who, if they once cried "Odds!" would have it odds through thick and thin. "I go," declared the squire, "to walk the earth henceforward with a plain foot, which, if it is not decked in a shoe of Córdovan leather, will at least not lack a hempen sandal."

Then the steward told him that, if he so willed it, he should depart, in spite of the grief they all felt at losing so worthy a governor; but that, as a governor, Sancho ought to render to the proper authority a full account of his government before leaving it. Sancho replied that he meant to do that, when he met the duke himself. He was then offered everything needful for his journey; but his desire was for nothing more than a little barley for Dapple, and a half-loaf for himself. So they let him go, with many tearful and affectionate farewells on both sides, and, upon their own parts, with much genuine admiration for the honest fellow's good sense.

Sancho came in time to the duke's castle again, rendered a full account of his adventures, and declared decidedly and continually that he had had more than enough of governments. And by and by, Don Quixote growing restless at the inactive life he was leading as the duke's guest, the knight and squire took a grateful leave of their host and hostess, and rode forth once more towards the city of Saragossa.

7

How Don Quixote was Overcome, and how he went Home

Although, as we know, it had been Don Quixote's first intention to ride to Saragossa, yet, upon the advice of some gentlemen whom he met a little later, he changed his mind and took instead the way to Barcelona. For there, he was told, some famous jousts were also to be held shortly.

He and his squire met with many adventures on their road; and more than once the knight urged Sancho to take the opportunity of lashing himself as he had promised, and so deliver the beauteous Dulcinea from her enchantment.

"Patience, my master," was Sancho's reply, "and consider, that to whip oneself in cold blood is a most cruel deed. All in good time; I keep my promise well in mind; let my lady Dulcinea be patient likewise, for, when she least thinks to see it, she shall behold me as full of stripes as a sieve is full of holes."

At Barcelona Don Quixote was very well received and entertained by a gentleman of the city, one Don Antonio Moreno, who had heard of the knight and his hare-brained doings. Don Quixote stayed at his house for several days; and then, upon a certain day, met with a grievous and overwhelming adventure which altered all the remainder of his life.

He had ridden out, fully armed, upon Rosinante, from the city early one morning, to take the air upon the seashore, when he suddenly beheld another knight riding rapidly towards him across the sands. The newcomer was armed from head to foot, mounted on a strong horse, and bore upon his shield a great white moon. As he came nearer he raised his voice and called aloud to the Don.

"Illustrious and valiant Don Quixote de la Mancha!" he cried. "Know me, for I am called the Knight of the White Moon, of whose far renowned exploits you must have heard. I come to do battle with you, to cause you to confess that the lady of my heart, whoever she may be, is ten times more beautiful than your Dulcinea del Toboso. The conditions of combat shall be, that if I vanquish you you shall lay your arms aside, and retire quietly to your own home where you shall remain, nor go in quest of any more adventures, for the space of a whole year. If you vanquish me, I am wholly at your mercy, my horse and my arms are yours, and all the glory of my deeds is thenceforward transferred from me to you. Give me your answer swiftly, then, for this affair must be begun and ended this very hour."

The Don was amazed at the stranger's words and his challenge; but he answered gravely and composedly that the beauty of the fair Dulcinea del Toboso was beyond question above that of all other ladies in the world: his challenger had surely never beheld her, he said, or he would not have uttered so false a statement

as he had just made. At the same time, he at once
accepted the challenge and the conditions set forth;
only, in the event of his being the victor, he had no
wish to receive the fame of the other's exploits, being
contented with his own, such as they were. "Choose
your part of the field, then, sir knight," he added courteously, "and I will do the same, and Heaven and St.
Peter bless the combat."

By this time many gentlemen of the city, including
Don Antonio and the city viceroy, had come to the
seashore, having seen the strange Knight of the White
Moon, and wondering whether this new adventure was
a jest, or in sober earnest, and also who the knightly
challenger could be. They were informed of the terms
of combat, and presently saw the opponents wheel their
horses round, and charge rapidly forward.

But the steed of the strange knight was far nimbler
and swifter than poor Rosinante. He and his rider came
on at full tilt, and, before Don Quixote had run two-
thirds of his course, met him with such a terrific shock
that our knight came crashing heavily down upon the
strand, Rosinante falling with him.

Immediately the Knight of the White Moon was upon
him, lance to throat, demanding the conditions of the
challenge, with a threat of instant death if he would
not at once confess them. But as he lay at the victor's
mercy, sorely stunned and hurt, Don Quixote, not having strength to raise his visor, replied faintly and hol-
lowly from behind it that Dulcinea was the most beautiful lady in the world, and he the most unfortunate

knight. "Now take my life from me, since you have taken away my honour," murmured he.

The life of the Don, however, was not, it seemed what the Knight of the White Moon required. The worshipful Don Quixote should live, he said and with him should live the fame of Lady Dulcinea's beauty, if he would yield to the conditions of combat agreed upon, and retire to his own village, there to dwell quietly for one year, or for as long as his conqueror should command. This, in the hearing of the city viceroy, of Señor Don Antonio, and of all the other spectators, the vanquished man promised to do, on the word of a true and honourable knight. Then the Knight of the White Moon, making the company a low bow, mounted his horse and galloped away at full speed towards the city.

Don Quixote, being lifted from the ground and having his helmet removed, was found to be white and shaking, and in a cold perspiration; whilst the hapless Rosinante was unable to stir. They bore the fallen champion back to the city and to his bed, faithful Sancho, full of trouble at this unlooked-for disaster, following him all the way, not knowing what to think or to do.

Don Antonio, meanwhile, curious to know the true name of the mysterious Knight of the White Moon, rode after him, and found him lodged in one of the city inns. There the stranger, at the gentleman's request, threw off his disguise and disclosed himself to be no other than the bachelor Samson Carrasco! He told Don Antonio all his story: how, pitying Don Quixote's craziness, he had set himself to vanquish him and cause him to return home; how his first effort had failed, yet his hopes of curing him finally had never dwindled; until at last he had happily got the better of him that day. He added, that he knew Don Quixote would most faithfully observe the promise he had made, and therefore he, the bachelor, and his friends, sincerely trusted that a right understanding might be restored to one who had originally possessed such a good one until those foolish notions of chivalry took so firm a hold upon his mind.

Samson Carrasco rode back, unrecognized, to his village; and Don Quixote, after having remained in bed for the better part of a week sick, shaken, disheartened, and brooding moodily over his defeat, set out for his home with Sancho. The knight rode Rosinante, who had painfully got upon his legs again, but the squire trudged afoot, for Dapple was loaded with the Don's armour.

As they departed from the city Don Quixote, passing the place where he had been overthrown in combat, gazed upon it with wistful melancholy "Here Troy once stood," he murmured. "Here my misfortunes and my feebleness robbed me of my fame; here the glory of my deeds was darkened; here fell my happiness, to rise no more!"

Sancho, much distressed at his master's sadness, comforted him with all the wise maxims he could find; and the two went on their way. Several strange adventures befell them before they reached their village; and one of the incidents that occurred caused the Don to make

a resolution to turn shepherd for a whole year after he got home and lead a pleasant pastoral life, as he imagined all shepherds did, in the woods and fields. But this plan was never carried out, for fate ordered otherwise.

On the way home, Don Quixote was most anxious that Sancho should now fulfil his promise of self-whipping for the disenchantment of Dulcinea, and he even offered to pay his squire in good coin of the realm for as many lashes as he should lay on. This caused the tardy Sancho to prick up his ears.

"Well, sir," said he, "the lashes I am to give myself amount to three thousand three hundred. If we price them at a quarter of a real apiece (and I will not take a jot less, though the whole world should order me) the sum comes to three thousand three hundred quarter-reals, and that, if you reckon it squarely, makes a sum of eight hundred and twenty-five whole reals. By your worship's leave, then, I will lay on in good earnest and take from your worship's money, of which I have charge, this sum named, neither more nor less. So I shall go home contented and wealthy, if well whipped; but yet I remember a saying of my granddam's— 'Trouts are not taken with dry hose and shoon,' and so I say no more."

The delighted Don thanked his squire many times for this promise; and the bargain was struck. And that same evening, when darkness fell, and master and man were encamped in a small wood off the high-road, Sancho made a whip of Dapple's halter, threw off his jacket and vest, and moved away amongst the trees to begin his lashing. His master anxiously besought him not to hurry himself, nor to lay on with too severe a hand; and the squire began, Don Quixote counting the strokes. But when six or eight had fallen upon his shoulders, Sancho began to think that this jest was too heavy and the price of it too light; might not the quarter-reals be made halfreals, he questioned?

"Proceed, my friend," replied the Don magnificently. "And I will double the pay."

"Away with it, then," was the triumphant answer, "and may it rain lashes, say I!"

Now the evening was dark, as we have said, and the heavy shade of the trees made it appear darker still, so that neither man could see the other. Crafty Sancho took advantage of the deep gloom, and, having no mind to flay his own skin, began to lash the tree-trunks instead, with much cracking of his whip and many heart-rending groans that made the wood ring again, and seemed to be tearing out his very heart-strings. On went the chastisement and the lamentations, until the tender-hearted Don could bear them no longer.

"Stay, stay, my son!" he cried. "You have already given yourself above a thousand lashes, if I have reckoned aright. Surely that is enough for the present. Heaven forbid that you should whip yourself to death for me, or even for the lady Dulcinea. Rome was not built in a day, remember; therefore I pray you to leave off now, and finish the business at another suitable time!"

"No, sir," came Sancho's voice out of the darkness, "it shall never be said of me: 'The money paid, the work delayed.' Go apart, dear master of mine, if you like not the sound of the whipping, whilst I give myself another thousand lashes or so, for two more such doses as I have forced myself to take already will finish the job completely." For the rogue was warming to his work, and his mind was on the handsome payment he was to receive.

The Don covered up his ears, and slipped away between the trees, whilst Sancho began to lash the trunks with redoubled vigour. He had stripped the bark from more than one tree, and had just thrashed a mighty beech with a tremendous stroke, crying at the same time: "Down with thee, then, Samson, and all that are with thee!" when his master rushed up again, and this time seized the halter and wrested it from his hands.

"Hold!" he cried loudly. "Shall I be the death of thee, my honest lad, and the cause of lifelong misery to thy wife and little ones? Nay, nay, let Dulcinea await another opportunity for the rest of thy whipping, until thou shalt have gained more strength, and canst bear it without fainting!"

Then Sancho, grinning to himself in the darkness, ceased his lashing, and allowed the Don to cover him up gently with his own cloak, in which he presently lay down and slumbered comfortably until day dawned. Upon the following nights the rest of his punishment was performed amongst more trees, greatly to the injury of their barks and the satisfaction of the whipper thereof, whose own back suffered so little from the lashes, that those he inflicted upon it would not have brushed off a fly.

And now, a day or so later, the two adventurers came to the summit of a low hill, whence, looking below them, they beheld their own village. At the sight of it Sancho knelt down in thankfulness and delight, crying: "O country long-desired, open thine arms once more to these thy wandering children! See thy son Sancho Panza returning to thee again after many dreary days, if not very rich, yet exceedingly well whipped. And see also thy illustrious son Don Quixote, who, though he returns conquered by another, yet remains a conqueror over himself, and that, as I have heard tell many a time, is the greatest victory of all!"

So they rode on into the village, where all the village urchins, the villagers, the priest, the barber, the bachelor, the niece, the housekeeper, and Sancho's wife and daughter, flocked out to behold them, to overwhelm them with questions, and bid them welcome home. They conducted the Don to his house, where almost immediately he went to bed, for he was in reality very ill, and greatly enfeebled, and at heart he grieved continually over the defeat he had suffered.

And whether it was this melancholy fretting, or the disappointment he felt at beholding no Dulcinea, disenchanted or otherwise, upon his return; or whether the many hardships and buffets he had encountered in his adventures had proved too much for his frame at last, none could tell; but a consuming fever seized him, and he never rose from his bed again. Six days he lay there, brooding often, and drowsing a great deal. In vain his friends tried to rouse him from his languid melancholy; in vain the doctors came and shook their heads and felt his slowly-weakening pulse; whilst his niece and housekeeper hovered about him weeping, and poor trusty Sancho never stirred from his side.

At length one day, after a long sleep of six hours, he awoke and said in a stronger voice than usual: "Heaven be praised for all its blessings to poor erring man!"

His niece came and bent over him. "What do you say, dear uncle?" she said; for it seemed to her that his speech was less wandering than it had previously been.

"Heaven be praised, I say," continued the Don, "for it has granted to me, in these my final hours, a clearer judgment and a sounder understanding. At last I see the folly of all the romantic notions I once had, which I know now were nothing but dreams and delusions, but which in former days were all the world to poor foolish me! Would that my days might be lengthened, that I might prove to the world how little I regard such delusions now! But that may not be. Dear child, call in the others, for I would fain make my confession and my will."

At that moment the priest, Master Nicholas, and Samson Carrasco entered his chamber; and holding out both hands to them he cried: "Give me joy, good friends, for I am no more that foolish knight Don Quixote de la Mancha, but plain Alonzo Quixada, as my parents named me!" Then he told them how his mind was clear at last, how he repented his folly, and how he regretted having wasted so many good years of life reading fantastic stories of chivalry, and trying to imitate them. The priest, who saw that he was sinking fast, sent the company from the room whilst he confessed him; then, opening the door again, he beckoned them in, to witness the dying man's will.

Amidst many sighs and tears, and Sancho's loud and heartfelt sobbing, Don Quixote settled his worldly affairs for the last time, making the priest and the bachelor his executors, providing well and lovingly for his faithful housekeeper and his no less faithful squire, and leaving his niece sole heiress of his land, money, and goods. Sancho and the bachelor made one more effort to divert his thoughts from dying and to turn them to the happy rustic life he had planned to lead; but the Don, looking at them very wistfully, said in a sad and even voice:

"Peace, my friends: look not for this year's birds in last year's nest. I was crazy once: I am in my sober senses now; once I was Don Quixote de la Mancha: I am now Alonzo Quixada, a dying man. Think of me as kindly as you once did, and I shall die content."

So his will was completed at last, and almost at once a fainting fit seized him; nor, in the little time that was left to him, did he recover consciousness for very long, and, finally, he ceased to breathe.

Thus died the famous Don Quixote de la Mancha, an honourable, kindly, and upright gentleman, who, whether as a romantic knight or as plain Señor Quixada, was ever beloved by all, and remains beloved to this day, by all succeeding generations who have heard his story.